A TWISTED TALE OF HISTORY

# P T BATEMAN

# THE WISHKEEPER'S REDEMPTION

## A Twisted Tale of History

For more information, or to book an event, contact: info@ptbateman.com
http://www.PTBateman.com

Editor: Lisa Kegley-Cloud

Book Cover design and Layout by Kristina Conatser | Captured by KC Designs
www.capturedbykcdesigns.com

Paperback ISBN: 979-8-9886281-2-5

*Scan QR to visit
the Author site and
learn more about
upcoming books
and events!*

# <u>Dedication</u>

*For those of us who constantly struggle with demons,
both real and perceived, there is hope.*

# CONTENTS

# CONTENT WARNING

This book contains graphic scenes of violence, non-consensual sex, torture, and gore. Please proceed with caution.

1

# GENIE'S BEGINNING

G enie sprawled out on his couch, the weight of time pressing upon his broad shoulders, unaware that this moment would mark the final stretch of his enduring prison. The large, ornate couch, an artifact of opulence that predated his residency, seemed to mock the limitations of his confinement. Even in his miniature form, Genie stood tall, a towering figure of over seven feet, his muscles sculpted over centuries of servitude. His meticulously trimmed goatee belied the detail-oriented routine he maintained to retain a semblance of humanity amidst his supernatural existence.

Yet, for all his efforts to appear human, the truth of his essence lingered in subtle deviations from the norm—a lack of legs and a blue hue that betrayed his supernatural origins. Confined to a space scarcely larger than a foot-long lamp, he pondered the paradox of spaciousness within confinement, a riddle lost in the mists of time.

But such existential musings yielded to the weight of his millennia-long servitude, a burden etched into the fabric of his being. Over two thousand years he had endured the whims of mortal masters, granting wishes with a begrudging obedience that smoldered with resentment. The memories of those wishes, some borne of envy and greed, others steeped in sinister intent, haunted his every moment. Even in slumber, the echoes of screams reverberated through his consciousness, reminders of the consequences wrought by his supernatural powers.

His gaze drifted to the memory orb, a relic he dubbed the Wishkeeper, a name he sometimes also referred to as himself, its translucent depths a repository of every wish granted. The thought of delving into its waters filled him with a primal dread, for within lay the chronicles of his servitude, including those of Jack, whose wishes bore the mark of darkness too profound to be ignored. Yet, he rationalized, they were not his wishes to bear; they were Jack's, and the burden of their fulfillment weighed heavy upon his soul, cutting him every time he thought of Jack to his very core. He involuntarily shuddered when he thought of Jack.

Pushing the residual thoughts of Jack and the others away, he got up. It was early morning; at least that's what his sundial had told him. Confined to this lamp he called home, he had no real way to tell the hour, the day, or even the year for that matter. The mystical movement of the sundial gave him some sense of normalcy though its shadows were only based on the light that came from a source not of this world. He was not of this world either, though he once had been. He growled at its presence.

The year was 651 B.C. Hasba, as he was originally named, had been playing a game with his friends in the hot desert sand. Their tent shielded them from the harsh rays of the sun. It was a friendly dice game with chips that the modern world would later refer to as Backgammon. At the time, he was just seventeen years old and considered a man in those days. His father had given him a house and land as a gift when he was just fifteen years old. He was labeled rich because he came from a family who bred Arabian horses for the kingdom. The Median aristocrats and rulers, including Deioces himself, paid his father well for the steeds. Hasba would take over his father's place as a horse breeder when the time came. He had also acquired one wife, Adlina, by this time and was about to wed his second when he came upon a strange lamp in the sand.

It was Hasba's turn in the game. He shook the dice in his right hand and then threw the dice. He must have thrown them a little too hard, and one landed well beyond the circle game area under the tent where they had been playing. He got up to retrieve the wayward dice and headed in the direction they were thrown. The desert wind had started to pick up, warning of an impending sandstorm, and he lost sight of the dice in a sandy dune. Reaching the mound, where he thought the dice had landed, he sat down. He dug his hands into the sand, trying to retrieve the dice before the storm hit. Scoops of the gritty substance flew into the air, twirling like mini tornados as he dug.

His fingers touched upon something solid. Thinking it was one of the dice, he reached his hand around the object. It wasn't the dice. It was far heavier and much bigger. Curious, he pulled the sunken object out. It was some round object but pointed at one end with a handle on the top. Encased in sand, he rubbed the surface to get a better look.

Suddenly, the skies darkened, and lightning lit up the clouds. Thunder rumbled through the sky. Sand pelted his face as he tried to cover his eyes. Before him, though he could not see it, a swirl of mist started to emerge from the object's tip, growing bigger as it ascended toward the sky. Eerie sounds coiled around him sending panic through his veins. He dared not look, but curiosity got the better of him, and he cautiously opened his eyes. He shielded his eyes as he tried to avoid the swirling sand. Strange images appeared to be dancing among the bits of sand. A large shadow began to come into focus.

Hasba scrambled backward away from the mysterious scene in front of him. He tried to gain traction in the sand but could not keep his footing. The mist spoke before he could turn over and place his feet under him.

"I am the all-powerful Genie," its voice boomed. "You are now my master. I grant you three wishes. What shall they be?"

Hasba froze and turned back to face the voice. The sheer size of this Genie, as it had called itself, was enough to make the bravest man tremble. Its voice was nothing like he had ever heard before. It spoke in a manner of power, purpose, and fear, all mixed in a way he could not comprehend. Even the rulers never commanded such attention and instant respect as this creature swirling before him.

"I do not understand." Hasba's voice cracked as he addressed the Genie. "Who? What...are you?"

"I am the all-powerful Genie," the deep and resonant voice said again. "I have the power to grant you three wishes—three things you desire the most, three of your wildest dreams, three of your most secret longings." The Genie ended his explanation with a deafening sound that shook the ground beneath Hasba.

Intrigued, yet still unsure and apprehensive of the apparition, Hasba contemplated the offer presented before him. He was a rich man, sure. But he could be richer, maybe even surpassing his father's wealth. Greed started to take hold of his thoughts. He had one wife and was getting ready to marry another, but he could have a hundred wives. His family bred exceptional horses, but he could ask for more land and more sires so they could breed dozens more, expanding their enterprise. So many things, wishes as the Genie called them, came to him. The possibilities were endless, and his excitement grew with each desire he thought of. But first, he needed to know what exactly he could and could not wish for, and if there were any conditions upon his wishes. His father was a shrewd enough businessman and had taught him that all business transactions have some conditions.

"How long do I have to make these wishes before the offer expires?" he asked. He wasn't as confident as he wanted when addressing the Genie.

*Maybe I should ask for bravery*, he thought.

"Depending on the time of day, you have until the moon falls or rises in the sky," the genie responded. Hasba thought he caught a glimpse of the genie rolling his eyes. He must have been asked this question before, although he had no basis for this theory. Instead of thinking of all the possible conditions the genie may have, Hasba thought it better to ask that question before he babbled on about any others.

"What are the conditions of these wishes?"

"You cannot ask me to kill someone, even your worst enemy. You cannot ask me to have someone fall in love with you, you cannot ask for more wishes, and you cannot ask to be a genie," the genie replied.

Hasba didn't even think about wishing to be a genie. But the idea started to grow inside his mind, and he couldn't think of anything else. It started to consume him. If he were a genie, he could do anything. He could acquire anything. He could grant himself wishes over and over, and the last wish he would wish would be for more wishes! He, a mere mortal, wasn't allowed to ask for more wishes, but as the genie...

The genie continued to swirl above Hasba. Casually, he crossed his arms, waiting for the wishes to come. He didn't seem impatient for the wishes to be granted. It was almost as if he was bored by the entire process. It was as if he could read Hasba's mind, knowing what he was thinking. Hasba tried to feign detachment from his desires, but it proved impossible.

"I wish to have fifty more wives," he blurted out. "I know you said you couldn't make someone fall in love with me. I don't need them to love me; I just want them to be mine!" He laughed at his cleverness.

"When you return to your home this evening, you will find fifty wives waiting for you," the genie simply stated. There wasn't any tone in his voice. It was stated matter-of-factly that he had granted this same wish over and over again. If Hasba was intrigued by the lack of interest the genie had shown when he granted the wish, he wouldn't have pursued the subject further.

"How do I know this to be true?" Hasba doubted that fifty wives were waiting for him to return home.

"A genie cannot lie," the genie retorted disgustingly as if he had been personally insulted.

Seeing as he had no choice but to accept the genie's word, he thought of another wish. He only had two left and not even an hour had passed since his discovery. He wondered if he should hold on to the other two wishes until he had more time to concentrate on what he wanted next. The more he thought he should be patient, the more impatient he became.

He thought about the wish he had just been granted and something struck him. The genie said, 'when he returned home.' Home. He could have the biggest palace in the area. His father would be jealous. His friends would envy him.

*Don't I need a bigger home, or rather, a palace, now that I have fifty wives?*

Greed took over his thinking. He wrung his hands in delighted anticipation of asking his next wish. No matter how hard he tried to save his wishes, he gushed out his next wish.

"I wish for a bigger house! One that will make the King himself jealous of its magnificence. I want it to be filled with precious jewels, the finest fabrics garnishing the furniture, and the most prized wines of the empire! I want the floors to be paved with gold slabs and walls so high the sandstorms wouldn't dare to enter! I want a room for every wife I have and more rooms for all the children they will bear me. I want servants to wait upon me and my family. I want all that as my second wish!" Hasba almost doubled over in the sheer delight of what he had just wished for. His gluttony had taken over all his reasoning. He only saw himself as the most powerful person in the realm. If he couldn't be the genie, he'd be the next best thing – the richest, most respected person in the world!

The genie unfolded his arms and proclaimed, "Your second wish has been granted. All that you have asked for awaits you when you return this evening." The genie bowed his head and sighed.

Though he was bound by the chains of the whims of man, secretly he hoped that one day, someone would grant *him* a wish, a wish for his freedom. Every time a new master released him from the confines of the lamp, a glimmer of hope would spark within him only to be dashed by the greedy, selfish wishes he was forced to grant. He was far from the one-thousandth person he must grant wishes to be free, but with each new master, he had hope. He hoped this one would grant his freedom, but he severely doubted it given the greed he saw in Hasba's eyes. The hope he felt when he was released was always replaced with anger as his freedom never came about. He loathed being kept in bondage.

Hasba returned home to everything he had wished for. Beautiful women greeted him at the gates of his new home. They swarmed him as if he was the richest man around, and given the palace, they found themselves in, they couldn't find any doubt in their assessment. The women were not overly loving towards him, just self-centered in their greed. They were dressed in the finest material of all colors. Their heads were crowned with jewels that matched their robes and fit snuggly around their waists, accentuating their figures. They all were young, about Hasba's age; ripe for bedding and creating the next generation of his line.

The palace he had been granted was overwhelmingly massive. Hasba stared in awe at its size. His eyes took in every detail of it. The walkways' glass-like stone, the brick structures' smoothness, and the golden ornaments that adorned the arches and courtyard. Giant columns with their tops carved into lions, bulls, and eagles surrounded the palace. All of this was his! Inside, his heart pounded at the excitement he had been granted. He wanted more, but he was down to his last wish.

*How can I get more from the genie?* He knew he couldn't ask for more wishes, but could he think of a way to trick the genie into that idea?

He pushed the women that had gathered around him away. They obediently left him. He needed to think. He walked briskly towards his quarters; an unexplainable instinct guided him to his rooms. Once inside, he closed the tall, dark wooden doors, shutting out the noise and distractions. Hasba stared at the enormous bed that was now his. A white silk curtain canopy encased the bed, which was covered in a soft, red, and gold overlay. Pillows sat fluffed at the headboard. He plopped down, his weight sinking into the softness. Hasba closed his eyes. All the excitement of the day had made him exhausted. He needed sleep to think of his next step in tricking the genie.

The genie quietly made himself known inside the room. Hasba awoke with a startle, feeling the genie's presence in the room rather than hearing him enter.

"How did you get in here?" he asked, still shaken by the genie's sudden appearance.

"I came in through the window," he explained nonchalantly as he wondered about the intelligence of the man who now held him captive.

Hasba shrugged his shoulders, feigning any ignorance of the genie's powers.

"What is your third wish?" the genie asked.

Hasba sat up in his bed and spoke quickly. "I need more time to think about my next wish. It is, as you said, my last one and I want to make it worthy."

"You must make all your wishes before the sun rises or the sun sets, depending on when I am released from my lamp. I find the movement of the sun to be most beautiful."

"You did not tell me that! I don't care about the beauty of the sun!" Hasba was taken aback by the genie's words. He needed more time to think and scheme. "That's not fair!" he exclaimed. "I didn't start my wishes until well after the sun rose today, and now it's almost dark! You must give me more time to think!"

"You must make your wishes between the two passages of light and darkness, whether it be the sun or moon that shines," the genie said again with frustration.

Hasba started to panic. He wanted more time, and he wanted more wishes. He got up from the bed and began pacing around the room. Having the genie hovering around was causing more anxiety.

"Leave me!" he shouted at the genie. "I will call you before the sun sets with my final wish."

With that, the genie simply floated back out the window from which he came, still within the sight of his anxious master. He hated *his* master for this obnoxious clause in the rules.

# 2
# HASBA

With the genie gone from his immediate sight, Hasba started thinking hard. He had two of his wishes granted; two very good wishes. But he wanted more. Most of all, he wanted the genie's power. Never again would he be given this opportunity to make something of his mediocre life. He had never heard of this genie legend. He wondered if any of his friends or family had. He briefly thought about asking them about it but thought better of it.

*What if they wanted wishes?*

He didn't have any intention of sharing this wonderful gift. This was his gift and his alone. Allowing anyone else to make this last wish was not part of the plan.

*The plan. What was the plan? How could I trick the genie?* Hasba pondered.

He must be all-knowing and probably had others try to trick him before. Hasba thought himself cleverer than that. There had to be a way for the genie to grant the wish without realizing he had been duped. *But how?*

As time ticked by, Hasba still hadn't devised a way to make the genie grant him more wishes. He saw the sky darken and knew he was running out of time. Exhausted, he threw himself back onto the bed. Then the thought hit him! He had figured out how to get more wishes so the genie wouldn't know he had been tricked.

He ran to the window and called out for the genie to come to him.

"Yes, Master?" The genie said as his mystical form came through the window. "Have you decided on your final wish?"

"I have," said Hasba smiling at his ingenuity.

"I wish to be you!" he blurted out. Hasba had found a way to trick the genie. The genie had said he could not wish to be a genie, but he had said nothing about wishing to be him!

The genie was stunned, but only momentarily. He had thought his new master a fool, and, with his final wish, the genie knew he was right. The fool figured out how to trick him. The fool would soon find out exactly what his final wish had done. The genie grew. His massive frame filled the space between the floor and ceiling. In a voice much louder than Hasba remembered, he bellowed, "Your wish is my command!"

Hasba became frightened and confused. With the granting of the other two wishes, nothing changed inside him. Now, he felt a sense of trepidation as his body started to tingle. His physical form appeared to be changing as well. His tan skin started to darken with a blueish hue. His clothes began to change into a flowy transparent robe of deep blue. Everything he saw when he looked at himself was becoming blue. He also started to grow. Frantically, he looked at the genie. The genie was no longer blue.

The genie stared in awe at Hasba's transformation. A sly grin passed his lips, and his eyes narrowed in twisted delight. He continued to watch Hasba in elated disbelief. By granting his last wish, a wish to become the genie, not any genie but himself, Hasba had set the genie free. He looked at his wrists. The shackles he had once worn were now encased around Hasba's wrists! He was free! Hasba had set him free without even realizing it.

"I take my wish back!" Hasba screamed in horror at the genie as the realization of his grave mistake set in.

"Oh, no." The once Genie sneered back at him. "You wanted to trick me into giving you more wishes. Your greed and lust for more power have done this to you, not me. Now, you will be trapped to do the bidding of those who find you. You will now be the slave, not the master. You wished to be me, well, now you are! If you had been pure of heart instead of filled with greed and lust, your mortal life would have continued. You would have had all you had wished for, for the remainder of your life. All you had to do was wish for one more thing or set me free. But no! You couldn't contain your quest for more! You, my friend, are your undoing!"

The previously enslaved genie started to run from the room in his now mortal form but stopped in his tracks. *The lamp!* His eternal prison lay on the floor where he had once stood. Hasba's transformation was almost complete. He decided to wait until it was finished. He watched in awe as Hasba's once-human body became an apparition. No sustenance. No soul. Nothing that looked human any longer swirled in front of the once genie. He suddenly remembered what the genie that made him had said to him when he was free.

*You who set me free must name me.* That was the final rule of his freedom. He had forgotten he was now human and could live as such for the rest of his mortal life. The once genie turned to Hasba.

"You who set me free must name me," he said. Hasba turned to him.

"You tricked me into becoming you, and now you want me to name you?" He spit at the once-genie. "How dare you ask anything of me!"

"It is the law. You must name me, for now I am mortal and will live as a mortal man. What was once yours, is now mine. You are doomed to live as you have wished. I will now be the Sultan of this place and keep your fifty wives. You can do nothing about it. You can also do nothing about the law. Name me!" He shouted to the transparent figure.

Hasba couldn't think. He was tortured by what he had done. He threw out a name just to be rid of the mortal man standing before him. A man who would now take over his life. His future. "You will be called Horus from now on. Now leave my sight."

As the new name of Horus left the lips of the new genie, the once Hasba, another transformation began. The new genie began to shrink. His form became more vaporous, like wisps of smoke swirling around a fire. The vapors gathered themselves together and moved towards the lamp.

Horus stood mesmerized by the movement of the vapors. Slowly, he realized what was happening. The new genie would become trapped in the lamp, just as he had many years ago. He picked up the lamp and gently pointed it towards the wisps, guiding them into it. As the last remnants of the vapors were sucked into the lamp, he thought he heard a scream of despair. Then, it was over. Silence enveloped the room.

After a moment, Horus regained his thoughts and quickly left the room. He had to hide the lamp before someone found it and released the genie. He was afraid that he would be returned to his old prison. He hurried down the gilded hallway out into the courtyard. The guards briefly looked at him as if he were a stranger, but ultimately let him pass. It was as if they could sense something was off, something strange, but after they looked at Horus, they disregarded their suspicions. Horus thought about the guards' hesitation, but only for a second before he rushed past them through the palace gates.

He went to the stables and grabbed the first horse he could find. It neighed at his sudden movements but quickly relaxed as if familiar with its rider. Horus mounted the horse and took off towards the desert. He had to hurry as the sun was coming up, and he didn't want to explain why he was out so early in the morning, lest they think him someone he was not.

He rode for about twenty minutes before he slowed his horse. The horse neighed nervously, sensing its rider's tension. Looking around, he saw no one. He had come to a stop in front of a large sand dune. He dismounted the horse. It began to stomp around, and Horus feared he would bolt, leaving him stranded in the empty desert. He calmed the horse and then grabbed the lamp from the side satchel. He started to dig into the sand. Much like Hasba had done when searching for his game dice. Horus wasn't looking for dice, though; he was digging so he could bury the lamp. He knew the desert would engulf the lamp with its constantly shifting winds and sand. He hoped it would never be discovered again. He was unsure if he could possibly be turned back into a genie if it were found by any of Hasba's relatives. He wasn't about to take that chance.

After digging for a few minutes, he felt he had dug deep enough to bury the lamp and avoid its unearthing soon. He gently placed the lamp into the hole, resisting the urge to throw it into the pit he had dug, and started to cover it up. He felt a slight twinge of remorse as he started to pile the sand on top of it. It felt like he was burying someone alive, even though he knew from experience that not to be true. He also knew what being a prisoner inside that lamp was like, but he quickly pushed those emotions aside. He finally had his freedom and wasn't about to give that back.

He finished covering the lamp and looked around again. The desert was still empty of any signs of activity. He had done it. Somehow, he was free. With the lamp buried, he erased everything he had been. He danced around the dune, kicking sand here and there. He had been so sure that Hasba wouldn't have granted his freedom, but he did. His overpowering desire to be all-powerful had been his ruin.

Realizing the lateness of the hour, Horus mounted the horse and trotted slowly back home. He wasn't sure what made the guards let him go, and it intrigued him enough to find out. Making his way back through the palace gates, the guards raised their hands in greeting.

"Hello, Master," they called out in unison.

Horus froze immediately. *Master?* Was he the genie again? He began to tremble, but the guards just smiled at him.

"May I take your horse for you, Master Horus?" one guard asked as he approached. Horus couldn't believe what was happening. After being granted his freedom, he took on Hasba's form as Horus. He was confused but delighted. To avoid raising any suspicions, he dismounted and gave the reins to the guard.

"Yes, thank you," he said, as he quickly left the guards before they realized who he was, or rather, who he wasn't. He needed to start acting his part, his new life that he possessed. He headed towards his room. *His* room. *His* palace. *His* new life. His new, *mortal* life.

3

# HASBA-GENIE

Hasba brooded around the confines of the lamp. He had been so stupid thinking he could outsmart the genie. He never did ask him his name, but later he found out that and a lot more information when he was visited by the genie who had made all the genies. He didn't have a concept of time until the magical sundial appeared, so he had no knowledge of how long he had been imprisoned. He spent many nights in sheer panic and disillusion as he contemplated how to escape. He had tried to push his way out of the lamp. He tried to wedge himself through the neck of the lamp. Once, he had even tried to burn his surroundings, foolishly thinking he would be rescued somehow. The fire extinguished itself, leaving no trace of damage. Nothing he tried released him from his predicament. He was stuck in this never-ending loop of granting wishes.

One day, he had been milling around when suddenly he heard a loud pop accompanied by smoke. Another genie stood in the middle of the room. His shape appeared once the smoke had dissipated. Stunned by the abrupt appearance, all Hasba could mutter was, "Who are you?".

"I am Divine-Genie. I am the genie who made all the genies. I am the one that cannot be undone. I am the one forever trapped in this eternal hell that you are now tethered to. You do not need to be afraid," his tone was soothing as if he sensed Hasba's trepidation. Part of him enjoyed the fear, frustration, and anger that swirled just below the surface of all the newly created genies. Their peril fed his soul. If he could possess such a thing. He kept his perverse satisfaction in check though. He enjoyed this part.

Hasba sat on the couch, staring at the shimmery presence before him. His mind swirled with a thousand questions, yet his mouth could utter none.

Divine-Genie sat down on a chair next to where Hasba sat. His features mirrored Hasba. He had the same blue hue, tail-like lower half, and shackles adorned his wrists. The only discernable difference was the air of confidence, one could say smugness, surrounding the elder genie. He patiently waited for Hasba to speak, knowing he was confused and eagerly wanting to ask many questions. He pre-empted the conversation, trying to put the novice genie at ease.

"I'm sure you're wondering just how you came to be in this predicament and what is in store for you," his voice summoning calm.

"Yes," was all Hasba could say.

"Well, let me see, how can I explain all this to you?" he began. "I'll start with me."

Hasba quickly sat up, ready to listen and, hopefully, learn. Maybe this Genie would be able to explain just how he could leave this entrapment he found himself in, although he had a dreaded suspicion that what he was about to say would not put his mind at ease.

*Maybe I could find another escape*, he thought to himself.

He quickly squelched the idea. He doubted this genie could be somehow duped as the other one had.

"I was created before time began—before the sand you walked on, before the people you saw around you, before the animals that roam the desert now, and before your father's grandfather. I know that's a concept most people cannot grasp, but it's the only explanation I have. I created my first genie over a thousand years ago. There have been quite a few more genies that I've created since then, but a vast majority of them have now been freed."

Hasba perked up at the words he spoke: *Freed*. So, there was a chance he could be rid of this confinement and return to his life. He had mistakenly freed the genie whose place he took, but he wasn't sure how that all came about. He didn't know how he could be freed, but the possibility of it excited him. He intently listened to what this genie had to say.

"A genie can be freed, you know?" He looked at Hasba as he remembered how he unwittingly had set the genie he found free. He searched this newly created genie's eyes and saw a speck of hope, only to be dashed when he continued his story. "That is, once they have either granted the three wishes of a thousand men. Or, this is a rarity, if one uses one of his wishes to free the genie. That rarely happens."

A thousand men? Three thousand wishes? Would someone use a valuable wish to free him? Hasba stared in disbelief and deflation at what he had just been told.

*My freedom could take an eternity*, he thought. *How could I possibly survive with my sanity intact that long? There has to be another way.*

The Divine-Genie did say that if someone granted his freedom with one of their three wishes, he could be released from his bonds, but he again remembered how greed took over his thoughts when he had been granted the wishes. It seemed almost impossible to imagine someone would selfishly throw away a wish to benefit him. He sighed heavily as the Divine-Genie continued.

"As you know, there are laws, or rather rules...obligations, that all genies must follow. I believe you heard them when you were granted your wishes from Akan-Genie. Akan was his mortal name before he became a genie. He, too, foolishly wanted the power of the genie he had found. You see, there have been many genies, and most have been created by man's selfish greed for more.

"Take yourself for instance. You could have had anything in this mortal world you wanted. From what I could see, you were off to a good start, but then, greed invaded your thoughts, and you were powerless to control it." Hasba cringed at his words.

He was right. He could have, rather, should have, just wished for one more thing. One more material thing. But he couldn't control his desires for more. And now, he was paying the price.

"You will not be able to escape this life until someone comes along who can push aside his greed," The Divine-Genie continued. "Push aside unnatural desires for power, for lust, for anything they could imagine. You will need to find a compassionate person to free you, or as I said earlier, grant three wishes of one thousand men. A powerful genie, or Wishkeeper as some have called us, is a treasure to be sought."

"Why would you want to create a rule that someone can simply ask to be like the genie granting them wishes? Why did you make it so easy to become a genie?" Anger was starting to build inside Hasba.

"Why would I stop it?" Devine-Genie asked. "It seems kind of selfish of you not to want me to create more genies. Why should I care how many genies there are in the world? I can never be free, so the more genies there are, the more company I have."

"You are the selfish one!" Hasba stood up and confronted the Divine-Genie. "You are the one with greed! You are the one who will never be freed because no one has ever wished for your freedom, and no one can! You insolent bastard!"

"Ha. Now you see why I would like to have more genies in the world. You, and the rest of them, are simply a reflection of me. I get to live, so to speak, through all of you." He sat motionless, unphased by the outburst. "I'll tell you a little secret," he leaned into Hasba. "I don't want to be freed. I like being all-knowing and all-powerful. I very much enjoy it when I create more genies. I feed on their greed," he sneered.

Divine-Genie finally stood up as if the conversation was finished and turned to face Hasba. His soft demeanor began to change. His bluish hue became darker. His facial features became more sinister as he stared into the novice's eyes.

"You will become just like me. You will come to love the greed of your wishers. You will want your freedom, yes, but the need for their lustful desires will overwhelm your need for your liberty," he sneered. With his final words, he left just as quickly as he had come.

Hasba-Genie, as he now came to realize his new name, just as Akan had become Akan-Genie, stared at the emptiness of the room before sitting back down on the couch. The memory of that encounter still bothered him. That day, he knew he didn't want to become like Divine -Genie; he only didn't know what he would become.

Hasba-Genie snapped out of his memory. It had been a long time since he had thought of Divine-Genie. He had changed so much since that encounter, most likely because of that encounter. After the Divine-Genie had left, he made a vow to himself that he wouldn't become so cynical. He wouldn't let greed take him over. He wouldn't let the desire for his freedom diminish. He would find a way out of this mess or bear his punishment with gratitude.

*Who knows*, he thought, *the very next person whose wishes I grant just very well may wish for my freedom.*

Oh, how naïve he was then.

The first time the lamp had been rubbed since his entrapment came unexpectedly. Hasba-Genie truly didn't know what was happening. What had seemed an ordinary, mundane day suddenly became the first day in his life as a genie. A new Master had found his lamp, and the genie made his first appearance.

In the darkness to which he emerged from the lamp, his eyes adjusting slowly, he took notice of his surroundings. His massive form towering over a man before him. The scenery was vastly different from when he became a genie. Stone structures surrounded him. Though they were different from the structures of his past, they still had a similarity. He looked around at white alabaster stones. He saw strange horses milling about, shorter than those he had had in mortal life. He didn't see any people, only the man cowering below. Somehow, he knew exactly what needed to be done, but he also wanted to find out where he was and what time he was in.

"I am the all-powerful genie!" He recited word for word the remaining dialogue of what had been spoken to him. He couldn't remember memorizing those words; they just came out of him.

The man below looked up at him in disbelief just as Hasba had when he first encountered Akan-Genie. He finally gathered the courage to speak. His words were a language Hasba had never heard, yet he understood him perfectly.

"Where did you come from?" the man asked. He was a big man, though he had a young face. He was covered in a white tunic cinched by a leather rope and wore strange leather straps on his feet.

"I am the genie of the lamp. You may call me Genie, for that is what and who I am." As he introduced himself, Genie suddenly realized he no longer thought of his given name. He had lost his mortal identity. He was now simply the genie. Not only that, he also had lost his mortal home because he had no idea where he was. "I came from the lamp in your hand. If I may ask you a question; where are we?" he queried.

"This is the town of Golgotha." The man before him seemed befuddled at the question. *What is this strange object before me?* The man wondered.

"Ah," Genie replied, as if what the man said made sense. He had no idea of the place the man just mentioned, but for someone to be all-powerful, he must appear all-knowing, except he wasn't. "And, if I may ask another, when are we?" He needed answers.

Divine-Genie had never explained this part of the process. He hadn't thought about how to tell where he was or how much time had elapsed.

The man seemed confused by the questions. He, himself, was grappling with what was happening. He didn't have time to think of this stranger's dilemma. How could one not know when they were? Still grasping at the reality of what was happening and since he wasn't sure what he was supposed to do, he answered the genie.

"We are at the time of the greatest empire. You are in the presence of a true and loyal soldier of the great governor of Judea, Pontius Pilate. My name is Titus, and you say I can have three wishes." He tried to get the genie back to the matter at hand. It slowly dawned on Titus what the genie had said, and as Divine-Genie had warned Hasba would happen, greed had planted a seed in Titus' mind.

# 4

# TITUS

Titus was not a man with many friends. He was probably the most hated person in town. He didn't care that others were jealous of him. He did his job precisely. He mastered every aspect of it, every skill down to a science. He was a favorite of Pontius Pilate, too. Titus was one of the very few executioners in town. He enjoyed his job immensely.

Ever since he was a boy, people thought him strange. He could tell his parents were frightened of him, but they tried to love him anyway. He would do things that made them fearful. Once, when he was about twelve years old, the family donkey had gone missing. The missing donkey was something not to be made light of because his family was not what was considered rich, but still had a respectable household. The missing donkey was only one of a few prized possessions the family had owned. Its disappearance was devastating.

Ignoring his family's pleas for him to help them find the donkey, Titus stayed in his room. He didn't need to be there when they found the animal. He knew what they would discover. His joy came from his imagination of how their reaction would be. The image of the horror on his mother's face when she found the mutilated donkey gave him great pleasure. A deep pleasure that radiated throughout his body. If the nosy head servant hadn't been around while all the other male servants were out searching for the donkey, he would have found the servant girl who washed the floors and satisfied the stirring in his loins.

He had had his way with her before, after finding a small-town cat to torture. Torture and mutilation stirred his desire for sex. Hard, brutal sex. He had found her on her knees, scrubbing the bricks outside his parents' bedroom. Her bent-over figure made his cock grow hard. She was in the perfect position, in his mind. Almost as if she was inviting him to take her. He abruptly put his hand over her mouth as he approached her from behind and threatened to whip her if she screamed. He lifted her frock over her back and hiked up his robe, exposing his fully grown cock.

He could still remember the fear in her eyes as he violated her innocence, pounding himself in her with each thrust until his release. Her consternation drove his passion further. The more she silently cried out in pain, the harder his onslaught was. He pushed her off him when he had finally finished, leaving her quietly sobbing on the floor and daring her to make a sound. It was probably why he enjoyed killing the donkey and thinking about how he had committed the act with his own bare hands. Its violent death aroused sexual desires and he needed the floor girl for his release. Since that couldn't happen, his right hand would have to release his need.

It hadn't taken long after that for Titus to find his dream job. He may have been young, but he was of the mindset that the Romans needed to control the area and follow through with the mandated executions. The Romans had a hard time finding soldiers to carry out the sentences. They were either off to war in so many areas already around the Empire or simply didn't have the stomach for the job. Many people in Judea, in the whole Empire, were being executed and the Romans had found the very tortuous means Titus thrived on. They called it crucifixion. Whatever poor soul that had been sentenced to die, and there were plenty of them around, would be nailed to two intersecting wooden beams. A simple beam would suffice if there were too many to be executed at one time. To prepare the person for this excruciating type of execution, the offender was laid flat on the beam. They didn't put up too much resistance since they had been brutally beaten before they were even given over to the executioners.

Once in Titus' skillful possession, the real torture began. He would lovingly talk to the barely alive creatures; his soothing voice almost gave them hope of a quick death. Almost. He would start the process by caressing their bruised and broken bodies, search-ing for the most tender areas. He would then drive his thumb into the flesh extracting a guttural scream. Pleasure coursed through his body, and he increased the pressure. Oh, how he wanted to thrust himself into their open mouths, but he controlled it. He'd get his release somewhere else.

As his pleasure grew, so did his cock, to the point that it was painful. He needed release so he quickened the killing. He picked up the heavy, blood-crusted stake and hammer and drove it through the ankle bones of the victims. Several times he had almost released himself onto the victims' helpless bodies as they cried out even louder. When he got to this point, he hurriedly finished nailing the victim's wrists to the beams. He preferred the beams to be crossed so their arms were outstretched. It slowed the death process down as they gasped for air with each passing hour. He would give them one last look, hearing them desperately plea for a quick death. Sometimes they begged for mercy. He simply smiled at them and turned away to find a girl, sometimes a young boy, with whom to take his pleasure. He especially loved the occasions when his own rape victims would scream the same way the person he executed had.

Titus continued his torturous deeds as he grew up. He perfected his execution styles. Once, after a rather gruesome execution, he joined his fellow deathsmen for a drink. He didn't particularly care for these men or their company, but they were shelling out the coin for the drinks, so he went along.

Their conversation bored Titus. All these men could do was complain about their work and how hard it was for them to push aside the screams of the prisoners. Titus could only think about how rewarding his job was. He thought of all the pleasure he got from his job; the pitiful pleas for mercy did not tug at his heartstrings, as they called it, as they did for the men with whom he shared a drink. Sympathetic emotions didn't stir him. No, he knew exactly what emotions surfaced with every pounding of his hammer.

After just one drink, Titus begged his leave, mumbling something about the need to get home and wash the grime and blood from himself. The men waved him on in understanding. Taking a particularly dark alley that stank of donkey manure, his foot kicked a small object. The rattling of the metal along the stone pavement caught his attention and he walked towards where the object had landed, bending down to pick up what he had struck. With only small amounts of light from candles in the windows along the alley, Titus tried to make out the object now resting in his hands. It was cold to the touch, yet had a warming sensation like a vibration of heat. He could barely make out the intricate carvings in the metal. He drew himself closer to a window to get a better look.

He used his sleeve to rub the dirt and scum from the metal. In doing so, a small cloud of smoke began to appear before him. It grew into the shape of half a man. He had released the genie. Now, standing in its presence, he heard him speak. After hearing his thunderous voice tell Titus of the fortunate opportunity of what this power had told him, he began to scheme, as everyone who had ever come across this exquisite prospect had in the past.

Titus took in his surroundings. Not wanting to be seen, he ran down the alley to a small hut that was used to store grain. The mystical genie floated alongside him.

# 5

# TITUS' GREED

Focusing now after the initial shock of seeing the apparition before him and now inside the hut, Titus' twisted mind started to work. He could not believe his luck. Three wishes being granted would save him a lot of time and energy. How many times had he wished for sharper tools to do his job or even a room full of partners to satisfy his sexual appetite. He didn't care if they loved him. He didn't even care that they wouldn't be willing. Resistance was the best part of his desire. He loved a good torment before he released himself; it made the act that much more pleasurable.

"I want a room filled with men and women," he blurted out.

The genie sighed and granted his wish. The room suddenly filled with ten men and women who seemed dumbfounded at finding themselves there. They varied in shape, size, and age. Some looked rather rich, while others looked as if they spent their nights on the streets of the town. They started chatting excitedly among themselves, trying to figure out how they had come to be there. Their conversations grew louder until, finally, Titus yelled, "Silence!"

The room immediately quieted. Some of the women grabbed one another's hand, trying to find some comfort in each other. One of the men glared at Titus and made a move towards him. A sliver of an object flashed in his hand as the knife blade flickered from the light of the candles. Titus turned to face his would-be assassin. A sneer formed on his lips as he drew his knife from his side and thrust it swiftly into the man's belly.

"How dare you!" Titus snickered as he twisted and pushed the blade further. The man groaned in agony as he fell to the floor. Titus removed the blade, the tip dripping the man's blood onto the floor. He whirled the knife around the room pointing at each remaining person.

"Anyone else want to try anything that stupid?"

The horrified men and women started to cry as they watched Titus silently. They didn't know what was going to happen to them. They didn't want to die, but they didn't know if that was a possibility or not. To them, Titus was like the rabid dog that skirted around the town until a soldier was brave enough to kill it. They wanted to get away from the sights before them. Before it was their turn. They were helpless and they knew it.

Titus' eyes fixed on a petite woman who appeared to be about thirty years old. At seventeen, Titus was ready to take on an older woman. Once, he had thought about having his way with his mother, but then thought twice about it. As much as he didn't care what she would think of him or do to him, he knew his father would kill him. He longed to suckle his mother's tit again as he took her. He envisioned her moaning with pleasure as he slid his manly cock in and out of her. The woman that caught his eye reminded him of his mother. If he couldn't have her, this one would have to suffice.

He called the woman to him, thrusting his lips to hers when she was close enough. She started to squirm in his embrace until she felt the sharpness of the knife prick her arm. She instantly froze in place. The look in his eyes warned her not to try to resist him. Titus began to strip the woman naked. He watched the tears form and then drop from her eyes. He quickly hardened at the sight and pushed her to the ground. Removing his pants, he stood above her.

"Please, no," her voice quivered in protest, but she was helpless to stop him.

"Oh, yes. I'm going to take you right here, right in front of everyone in this room, right in front of you, too, Genie." He turned and glared at the genie. "And there's nothing you can do to stop me."

Genie could only watch in horror as one by one, Titus thrust himself upon the captives. His thoughts were in turmoil; he was paralyzed to intercede. He needed to find a way to stop this madness. A way to turn Titus' attention away from his actions. But how? These innocent ones could not escape as Titus brutally raped them. Many scrambled to cower in the corner of the dark room once Titus had finished with them. Soft whimpers echoed in the dark. The shame and humiliation apparent on their faces illuminated in the soft glow of the candles. This needed to end.

Titus finished with five before he stopped to catch his breath and strength. He didn't bother to dress as he slid from behind his last victim. His body was covered in sweat and bodily fluids glistening in the soft glow of the candles. His breath was labored from the exertion. His eyes were wide from the satisfaction and the anticipation of finishing the other five. He hadn't been too selective in which one he chose first or what he did to them. Man or woman, he didn't care who he had his way with.

The genie could not stop him and could only watch in dread as Titus carried out his deeds. Genie tried to close his eyes and ears to the sounds of the scene unfolding before him. He wished he could leave this place and return to his lamp. He couldn't bear this. This was not what he had expected. He thought that granting wishes would be fun, even adventures like it was for him...before greed took hold.

Maybe he could remind Titus of the rules of the three wishes. Even if it temporarily delayed his vicious acts, the genie had to do something.

"Master," he called, distracting Titus enough to turn and face him. The impact of seeing Titus so hyped on his own lust sent shivers down Genie's spine.

"Master," he started again, "You must complete your wishes before sunrise. You don't want to waste the remaining two by staying here all night, do you? The sun will rise in just a few hours," the genie offered, trying to sound sincere.

"Ah, yes. Your senseless rules," Titus said as he gathered his clothing and covered himself. "Fine. I wish for this scum to be removed from this place so I can think of my next wish." Titus absently waved his arm around the room. The people disappeared instantly, much to Titus' surprise. It took a moment for Titus to realize what he had just done. He had inadvertently used the word wish.

"You tricked me!" he shouted at the genie, spinning quickly to face him. He picked up his knife, filled with rage, and lunged at the genie. His weapon did not affect the Genie as it harmlessly impaled the vapors of the Genie's form. Titus continued to thrash at the Genie until his arms grew tired. Exhausted, he dropped the knife and faced the Genie, his shoulders slumping forward; his knees almost buckling beneath him as they burned from the previous overuse of their energy.

Genie could not help but triumphantly grin at Titus' mistake. He felt relief that he had been able to stop the repulsive acts Titus had seemed so enthralled to commit. He also didn't feel deceitful in allowing Titus to waste his next wish. However, he knew Titus would not fall for any more deceptions.

Titus paced angrily around the room. He could not believe he had been so gullible. How could he have let this genie trick him? He was a smart man.

*Yes*, he thought, *I am a man. I am a cruel man. How I wish I could tear the genie from limb to limb.* He dared not say that out loud for fear the genie would sucker him again and he'd be out of wishes. He needed his last wish to be the best of them all. Something that would stay with him long after the genie had evaporated back into his lamp. *But, what?* He wondered. *What do I need? What do I want?* He struggled to consider his next wish.

Titus thought about a man he had heard of from Nazarene who was set to go to trial before Pilate. Someone whom the locals had thought to be their Messiah. He had seen many of these so-called Messiahs. They had come and gone like their precious lambs to slaughter as a sacrifice to their god. This one, though, made Pilate nervous. Pilate's wife had had a dream of this man. A dream where Pilate himself would cause this man's demise. A warning, the dream revealed, that Pilate's wife told him about. She had pleaded with him not to get involved. But, like most men of his time, he brushed aside his wife's nonsense. He was the Governor of Judea. Ceaser put him here because he had the confidence and demeanor to settle down the local religious fanatics and their hype over their perceived messiahs. He had wanted Pilate to bring peace to the area, no matter the cost.

Even though Titus was younger than most men in Pilate's court, Pilate had hand-picked Titus for his squad of execution-ers. Titus' reputation had become well-known in the area. Pilate himself didn't particularly relish having to sentence the people to death, but it was better than carrying out the deed. He could wash his hands of it all in the end. Per Ceaser's orders, and to cause fear in the populous, executions needed to be performed in the most brutal fashion to send a message that Rome would not tolerate any insubordination.

Titus turned his thoughts back to the man from Nazarene. He knew that the locals were going to have to make a choice between him and another man who was a thorn in the Roman's and Pilate's sides. A man named Barabbas. He was an insurrectionist; a man who loathed the Romans. Titus hated the man. The Romans would love to be able to put him to death, but Pilate was going to have to make a choice to appease the crowds and pardon one of them. It didn't matter to Titus who was pardoned because he knew the loser would be subject to the scourge that came before the crucifixion. He wanted to be the one who carried it out.

All Roman executioners were given their own tools to per-form their duties. Titus, however, was still too new to have the best of these tools. He got the leftovers—the tools no one wanted because they had been used so much. They were dull and worn. Though still able to do the job, they didn't have the flare of a newer tool. There was one tool he had seen used and the one he wanted most of all. It was called a flagellum.

A flagellum was a short whip consisting of three leather ropes, or thongs, attached to a handle usually made from an animal bone. The handle was probably made this way to instill terror in its victims. Knotted along the leather thongs were slivers of metal. The metal bits were designed to rip the skin from the recipient, causing long gashes when they struck. The prisoner, or convict, would bleed heavily from these wounds but not so they would die immediately. That would defeat the purpose of the torture. The Romans wanted to make examples of these prisoners in public, so the scourge would just be enough to bring them near death and they would be too weak to resist for long once they were nailed to the cross.

Thinking of all he could inflict with this new device; Titus slowly turned his narrowing eyes to the genie. His lips curled, showing his teeth. In a guttural growl, he made his final wish.

"Genie, I wish for a flagellum. Not just any flagellum, mind you. Oh, no. I want the handle to be made not of animal bone but the leg bone of martyr John the Baptist, as he was called. I want the leather thongs made from the donkey this so-called Messiah rode into Jerusalem on. I want the metal to be sharper than any known sword. This is my final wish."

Titus stood proudly in front of the genie and watched as the heinous wish seemed to twirl in the genie's thoughts. Titus could see the genie struggle with what he had requested. He could see the turmoil, the anguish, and the utter torment in his eyes, and Titus seemed to savor every drop of it.

Genie dropped his head in defeated sorrow. Divine-Genie never divulged to him that he would suffer like this.

*Am I fated to do the bidding of these types of men for eternity?*

He was helpless to stop what Titus was about to do. He was relieved that this was his last wish. He didn't think he could bear witness to the man's torture by Titus' inflictions, knowing he had played a part in it.

"I grant you your final wish." The flagellum appeared in Titus' hands exactly as he described it. He jumped with glee at the new device. He barely noticed the genie gliding back towards the lamp. He only caught the last wisp of blue vapors as they appeared to be sucked into the confines of the genie's eternal prison. Mesmerized, he watched the last of the genie disappear.

After waiting to see if the genie would reappear, Titus scooped up the lamp and left. The genie tucked safely back into the lamp he carried under his garments, he walked down through the alley, passing the storage building of all the artifacts Pilate had accumulated as payment from the townspeople. The structure held precious pieces of gold and silver. Plates, bowls, crowns, everything of value laid in piles as payments of taxes. Titus casually tossed in the lamp among the gathered treasures and thought no more of the genie.

# 6
# GENIE'S FATE

Genie collapsed as he finished entering the lamp. He lay motionless on the floor having no strength to move. He wished his thoughts would stop moving as his body had. But they didn't. He replayed in his mind all that he had witnessed with Titus. The screams of his victims resonated in Genie's head, pounding like drums, getting louder and louder. He let out a harrowing scream trying to drown out theirs. If only he could scream out all the horror he had seen, hoping beyond hope, the memories would evaporate with the sounds. They did not.

Genie was in utter psychological torment. "No, not Genie, I am Hasba!" he shrieked. He got up and paced around the room, holding his hands to his ears praying that would stifle the cries. It did not. He continued this activity for a long time until he suddenly stopped and noticed a new addition to the table in front of his couch.

Curious, he sat down and stared at this new object. It was a small glass sphere, no bigger than his palm. A black glass ball sat atop a support of three prongs of pewter. Looking inside this dark orb, he saw swirls of light—tiny white specks floating softly through the darkness.

Hasba felt a warming sensation in his temples. He closed his eyes, comforted by the soothing softness of the heat. Then, he began to feel a tug, as if something inside his head wanted to come out.

Very slowly and painlessly, the thoughts of Titus escaped from his temple. The horrible memories of all he had seen became a white wisp detaching from his mind. No longer did he feel the torment. No longer did he feel guilt. It was as if all the horrific images faded from him. He watched as this wisp, full of abominations, gravitated towards the orb. As soon as it touched the glass, it disappeared inside.

Hasba was left with a sensation of peace. He closed his eyes and sighed. Thoughts of the time he spent with Titus made Hasba suddenly realize the gap in time. He had been so focused on his first interaction with men in his new form that he overlooked the space of time that had taken place. It was centuries since he became a genie! His family was gone, long dead. He was overcome with grief and guilt. Gone was the father he so naively wanted to replace. The man he had looked up to. Who taught him the skills of being a master horse breeder. A man who was generous with his sons. A man who had been building a legacy for his children to inherit. Hasba wondered who took over his father's estate once he had passed. His brothers would have made excellent businessmen and breeders. They understood the hard work and skill in breeding horses so prized that even the Sultan asked for his family's horses by name.

He wondered if his mother was heartbroken when they couldn't find Hasba. His sudden disappearance must have been devastating for her. Did she silently weep over her lost son? Or did she push down the sorrow and lavish the love and affection Hasba had so callously discarded on her remaining sons? He wondered if they spoke of him during the evening meals. His mother used to give him extra bread because she thought him too thin for his age. He wondered who she gave the extra bread to now. Did existence fade away from their memory like the sands of the desert would brush away the tracks of its travelers?

His greed put him in this predicament.

*I could have easily thrown the lamp away instead*, he reflected. *Easy to say now*, he thought, *but not so easily executed.*

His inability to turn from such potential showed him he still had much to learn.

As he sat there, recuperating from the trauma, and lamenting in his sorrow, he heard the familiar pop and flash break the silence of the room. Divine-Genie appeared before him again.

"So, how did you like your first wishes?" His tone was condescending and abrupt.

"Why didn't you warn me?" he exasperated as he lay in utter exhaustion on the couch.

"Oh, why would I take my enjoyment away? Do you know how long it has been since I've watched one of my creations suffer?" he snorted. "I have very few pleasures in life, but watching you and my others suffer, is high on my list." His haughty tone raked Hasba's nerves.

"I can't do this for another nine hundred and ninety-nine people!" Genie exclaimed.

"It's the law. Unless one of those creatures releases you from this lamp and grants you a wish for freedom, you have no choice. I told you before, that your greed brought you this fate. I just facilitated it. You are responsible for this destiny, not me."

"But how do I deal with the torment when I grant these wishes? The laws are not so clear. I thought you said that I couldn't grant a wish to kill someone?" He felt as if Divine-Genie slapped him in the face at the mention of his past greed.

"And you didn't kill anyone. Titus did. You have no control over what they do with a wish if it is granted to the letter of the law. What you granted to Titus was only a tool, what he does with it is no concern of yours. What he did with those people was no concern of yours either. It was his greed and lust that drove him to those hideous deeds. Although I will say, I enjoyed watching it even if you didn't." He shrugged his shoulders in indifference.

Hasba could not believe this! How could the Divine-Genie not be affected? "Does that have something to do with your inability to empathize with those innocent people?" he said, pointing to the orb.

"Well, not having to relive those memories does help. The orb simply holds them away from your memories. You can revisit any memory that is contained inside. You have to ask it to reveal those you want to remember."

"Why would I do that?" Hasba asked incredulously. "Why would anyone want to do that?"

"Oh, I don't know. Because it's fun." Divine-Genie toyed with Hasba's emotions and torment, and he thrived on it.

Hasba glowered at Divine-Genie. He felt trapped, and he was. Trapped in this infuriating hell without the possibility of escape, given what he had seen in Titus, he doubted someone would willingly give up a wish to free him. It was an unbearable fate he found himself in.

"Leave me," he whispered, unable to continue this conversation.

"I will leave you, but you need to know something else before I go. Stop trying to maintain your old life, name, and ways. You left all that behind. Stop thinking you're still Hasba - *you're not.* You are simply Genie. I saw how you struggled to maintain your old name with that man, Titus. The title "Genie" comes along with the punishment. You are nothing but a servant now. A slave to mortal men. I will leave you. You will not see me again until you are freed. And, with what I've witnessed through mortal men, that will be a very long time from now."

*Genie. Not Hasba. Not Hasba-Genie.* As he now must think of himself, Genie wondered if what Divine-Genie said was true. He was truly lost to his previous life. He was doomed to an eternity of torment granting wishes to humanity. Was mortal man so vicious to one another that he was doomed to witness the atrocities indefinitely?

"Just one more thing," Divine-Genie said, bringing Genie's attention back to him. "I really shouldn't let you in on this little secret, but against my better judgment, I will. I noticed you had a hard time figuring out where you were and what time in history you had been summoned to. It's very simple to establish all that. Instead of asking the one who beckoned you from your lamp by rubbing it, you only have to touch their forehead. You will instantly know their thoughts and then determine where and when you are." With that, Divine-Genie popped and flashed from sight.

With Divine-Genie gone, Genie didn't know what to do now. It seemed as if the time he had become a genie until Titus was only a minute in his mind, but he now realized nearly half a century had passed between the two events. How long would pass before someone found his lamp? He had no way of knowing what Titus had done with it. Later, he would find out, through his other times granting wishes. The knowledge from those he would touch would show him the past.

Another object magically appeared in his room. A sundial. He stared in amazement at its sudden appearance. Then, he wondered how it was going to help. It was as if Divine-Genie was playing another cruel joke, and he was the brunt of it. The dial cast a shadow on its base. This gave him little comfort. Over time, he would come to learn, it became maddening. It was just another reminder of the time passing as he sat and waited, longing for his freedom. Or that wishes must be granted between night and day.

With time having no meaning, it didn't take long for another stirring of the lamp. Genie had no control over his staying or leaving or how much time had passed. He tried to remember what Divine-Genie had told him about figuring out the time in which he would emerge. It was dark again. He muttered to himself, "Why couldn't I be found in the daylight?"

He emerged to a pungent smell hanging in the darkness. It smelled of blood, sweat, and gunpowder—scents he was both familiar with and unfamiliar with. The sharpness of the gunpowder caught his attention. It smelled of smoke, saltpeter, and coal mixed together. Genie's eyes burned from it all, and the smell almost made him gag.

He towered above the man below him. "I am the genie of the lamp. I grant you three wishes..." He finished his mandatory guidelines. He didn't know just how much he wanted to take those words back, but he was about to find out.

Calmly, without any hesitation or fear, the man below, dressed in strange armor, looked up to the mysterious figure floating above him and boisterously said, "I am Vlad. You have blessed me well in this moment." The grin on his face was becoming all too familiar to Genie. He knew again that this stranger before him would not be the one to grant his freedom.

# 7

# VLAD

The undaunted man standing firmly before Genie was tall with long, black hair, caked in blood and grime, that hung just below his shoulders. He sported a mustache that grew almost to his cheeks and a puff of hair just below his lower lip. The well-formed muscles in his forearms could be seen under the cover of dirt and blood. His sword was clasped in his right hand, its tip barely touching the ground, but Genie could tell, it had been recently wielded as it was covered in blood. His appearance was unfamiliar to Genie, although certain characteristics, like an air of egotism, were recognizable. Steam rose from his body in the cold air.

A heavy rain had just passed through and muddied the bloody battlefield only yards away from where they were. Genie heard the sounds of men screaming in agony as blades cut into their flesh, and others screaming in triumph as they wielded their swords against them. The air was heavy and hung with the metallic smell of blood and steel. Half a moon hung in the sky, obscured by the smoke and steam from the weapons and bodies scattered throughout the battlefield.

Genie remembered what he had been told and stretched out his forefinger to touch the man's head. Drawing back from this intrusive invasion, Vlad raised his sword and sliced through the apparition. He swung his sword repeatedly, trying to destroy Genie, but to no avail. Genie's form re-materialized with each swing of the blade. Exhausted, Vlad finally lowered his weapon.

Again, Genie reached out his finger. This time he was able to touch Vlad's head. Instantly, Genie lurched back from the poisonous memories of this man. His frame began to reel from all the horror he was seeing.

With his finger pressed firmly against Vlad's head, the first memory to emerge was that of Vlad as a young boy. He was about eleven years old and standing in front of a man sitting on a throne-like chair. The man's head was wrapped in a white turban, his equally colored robe adorned in gold stitching. The chair he sat on was also adorned in gold statues and filigrees. The floor was covered in marble that glistened in the sun streaming through the massive windows. Pillars of white plaster vaulted throughout the room from floor to ceiling. This was the palace of Sultan Murad II. The Sultan was not a man to be taken lightly. He had spent many years trying to obtain his status through many military endeavors. He was not about to give up his throne easily again. He had obvious disdain for the two boys cowering before him.

Vlad's father thought it best to appease the Sultan of the Ottoman Empire by sending his two youngest sons to the Ottoman Sultan Murad II. Having previously defended the Holy Roman Empire against the Sultan, he felt that by sending Vlad, along with his younger brother, to the Sultan, he would send a signal that his family now supported Ottoman policies.

Vlad had been treated poorly by the Sultan and his soldiers, as Genie could see. He had been fed the scraps of food left over from the vast parties the Sultan held—scraps that even the dogs that roamed freely about the palace wouldn't be fed. He had many days when even the scraps of food weren't tossed his way. His treatment by the Sultan lasted six years. He vowed not to die then and would exact his revenge one day.

Six years later, Vlad was allowed to return to his home in Walachia. Upon his return, he found out that the nobles of his homeland had executed his father and older brother. The murderers did not like that his father had sided with the Ottomans. The now-open position caused a stir among those wishing to advance their status. Vlad decided to take his father's place as Governor of Walachia. It was a long, grueling campaign. He not only had to fight the members of the city, but he also had to fight his own younger brother who thought he should rule in his father's place since Vlad had, in his opinion, been tainted from his years in service to the Sultan. Vlad's prison sentence did not make him weak. He excelled in the environment, not only physically but mentally.

Vlad developed a taste for torture as he had to scrape for food at mealtimes. The guards would toss food at the captives, then stand back and watch in amusement as they beat at each other, trying to retrieve mere scraps of rotten food. Vlad had learned to be quick and beat his opponents to the strewn morsels. He was careful, though, as the prisoners held some value with the Sultan. He would fight the other prisoners in a way that left no bruises or markings. He had seen a man whipped within inches of his life for breaking another prisoner's arm in a scuffle over a piece of bread. He would have liked to torture them more but feared the Sultan would have him whipped. Instead, he honed his skills with the vermin that occupied his room at night. At first, he captured the scurrying creatures and snapped their necks. Then, his passion for the art of killing grew. He would impale them with any sharp object he could find, watching them writhe in pain. Their tiny squeaks of torment satisfied Vlad's suppressed lust for torture that could not be conducted on the other prisoners.

One memory stood out in Vlad's consciousness. Vlad had been in a battle with the Sultan. The Sultan felt his prisoners, unwilling guests, should fight in his battles. Prisoners dying in battle were useless to him as long as his own loyal fighters did not. Vlad refused to die fighting someone else's war, so he excelled in battle. After any victorious battle, many stakes were erected throughout the battlefield. One by one they would be driven into the ground next to the bodies of those that lay dead or mortally wounded. A practice Vlad perfected when he obtained his freedom later in life. The dead offered no resistance, but their impaled presence would be seen as a deterrent by those who were tempted to take on the Sultan in war. As the half-dead foreign soldiers were hoisted from the ground and then impaled on these stakes, Vlad had sat and ate his lunch at a table brought out to him amid all the carnage. He filled his belly with meats and cheeses that had been brought to him from the rations carried by the Sultan's food bearers. He dipped his bread in the blood that poured from their bodies as they slowly died in front of him. Their painful screams fell on unconcerned ears.

Not able to witness any more memories; Genie removed his finger from Vlad's temple. He had seen enough. So much death. So much torment inside this young man standing beneath him. He could feel the man's rage from all that he had endured, but he also felt a need for love, for tenderness that he had been unable to receive being his father's sacrificial pawn. Genie could not find any memories of a mother. A mother may have been able to reach this poor soul. She must have died before Vlad could produce memories of her. Genie felt a small pang of sorrow for the man.

Pulling Genie out of his woeful thoughts, Vlad spoke. His unconcerned demeanor at Genie's presence was puzzling.

*Did this man truly have no fear?* Genie wondered.

"So, you say I have three wishes, eh?" Vlad had been calculating his advantage while Genie had been prodding his memories.

"Yes, Master. Three wishes of whatever your vile heart desires except for the ones I spoke of." Genie answered.

Vlad ignored Genie's quip. "Well, as you can see, I'm in the middle of a battle here. I have every intention of winning this battle. You say I can't have you kill anyone, right? But I need to defeat these men. This battle must be won." His fatigue was apparent. He had been fighting this battle for over four hours now. He was not ready to retreat. But he wasn't sure how much longer he could fight. Finding his remaining strength, he recited his wish.

"I wish to win this battle." He roared, thrusting his sword over his head. At once, the men fighting on the battlefield found their aim suddenly true. No arrow missed its mark, and no ball catapulted shattered on impact with the castle he was trying to enter; they miraculously smashed through the stronghold. His men rapidly advanced towards their enemy.

Even as he watched his men, Vlad couldn't believe his fortune. He thought back to when his general had given him this lamp as part of a bounty Vlad had intended to give the noblemen of Walachia to try to win them over for his father's title. It had been a beautiful trinket added to the chest of gold and silver pieces. Fine jewelry with precious stones was also among the loot intended for the bribe. The noblemen turned their noses at the treasure and laughed at Vlad's request for governorship when he presented them with the bounty. Vlad had left the men and started to plot his revenge. They would soon regret their decision.

He had taken the chest as he exited the castle. Once back at home, he started using the spoils to build his own secret army. The lamp: he kept. There was something about it that had intrigued him. According to his major, who had found it among the ruins of a peasant's home he had come across while traveling throughout Romania, the lamp had been rumored to possess luck for those who held it. The home from which it was found appeared to be burnt and ransacked, but the lamp was not taken in the looting. It had been buried among the soot and burnt beams of the structure with only a tiny hint of shininess catching the sun in the early morning. The major inspected it as he picked it up. It was very dirty, so he placed it in his satchel. He would wash it when he got back home. He thought by giving it to Vlad, the two of them would be able to convince the nobles to grant Vlad his father's post.

During the battle, when there was a lull in the fighting, Vlad pulled the lamp from the satchel hanging at the saddle of his horse. His general had cleaned it thoroughly with soap and a brush, bringing out its magnificent sheen. He had been careful not to touch it with his bare hands. The general was a very suspicious man, and the legend about it had made him nervous as he cleaned it. Vlad held it in his bare hands, rubbing the sides for good fortune in the battle he had found himself in. That is when this genie appeared, and Vlad's luck truly had changed for the better.

Now, with the power of this genie by his side, he would not lose this most important battle and would finally claim his rightful position. He would no longer beg and grovel at the nobles. In fact, he started to plot how he would exact his revenge on them for the suffering they had caused him.

Pushing aside the thoughts of his newly acquired power, Vlad realized that the battle he and his men were fighting was over, and he had won. Several prisoners were taken and brought before Vlad to decide their fate. As chance would have it, two of the noblemen who had scorned Vlad were among the captives. Vlad examined the lot before him. About a hundred men were cowering before him, begging for their lives. Ignoring their all-too-late pleas for mercy, Vlad turned to his men.

"Men," he addressed his battle-worn, but victorious crew, "I want to show the nobles of this land just how powerful I can be. I want them to know that I will no longer cower before them. I will no longer be a subject of their jest and scorn. I will no longer tolerate not being given what is legitimately mine. They, now, will be in fear and awe of me!"

Vlad's men raised their swords in salute and hefty shouts of agreement. He sat on his horse and rejoiced in their praise. Pride and greed swelled deep in his core. Genie noticed it immediately, lowered his head, and softly shook it back and forth.

"Take all of these men except these two," he said pointing to the nobles he had recognized in the crowd. "I want these two to come with me. The others, I want to be impaled on stakes spread across the battlefield, but close enough to the castle that anyone entering it will look out and see the punishment for daring to confront me and take back what is mine!" he shouted.

His men stared in horror at what they had just heard. It was their first time fighting with their newly-found leader. Though they were victorious and shared in the triumph, they wanted to rest and prepare for the next battle. They did not share their commander's lust for more torture. The men started to mumble among themselves, unsure what to do. Vlad noticed their hesitation and dismounted from his horse. He grabbed one of his soldier's spears, turned towards one of the captives, and drove it through his belly, piercing him clean through to his back and beyond. He then hoisted the man up with the spear, still screaming in pain and agony, and slammed the bottom of the spear into the blood and mud-covered ground.

It didn't take long for the prisoners to realize their fate and they started to run. They tried to scramble away from Vlad's men in the slippery terrain, falling only to try to get back up covered in crimson dirt and grime. The sheer terror of their commander drove them in every direction, but Vlad's loyal men were faster encircling the would-be deserters atop their surefooted horses, holding them in place. They now understood their assignment. They could either do what their leader said or die the same way as their battle mate. One by one, each reluctant soldier grabbed a man, thrusting their spears just as their leader had, methodically impaling them to the ground. The two nobles that were spared were tied at the wrists by a long rope attached to the pommel of Vlad's horse. Vlad mounted his horse and slowly made his way into the fortress he had just captured. As he rode from the battlefield, he delighted in the screams behind him and the men scrambling to keep pace.

# 8
# VLAD'S REVENGE

"Genie!" Vlad bellowed as they reached the castle. "I wish for a chamber set up in the bowels of this wretched castle. I want it filled with a brazen bull, a breaking wheel, and a blood extractor. I want them in that room by the time I arrive in the next ten minutes!"

Genie glanced at the two men who had heard what Vlad had just commanded. He saw the horror and fear of his order projected on their faces. There was no denying the misfortune that would be bestowed upon them. When first captured, they knew that they would most likely be killed; they had no inclination that sadistically vicious torture would precede their death. Until now.

Against every fiber of his being, Genie had no choice but to grant the second wish. He guided Vlad and the prisoners to the evil room he had just created. Everything Vlad had wished for was set up throughout the room. To one corner sat the breaking wheel. Its victim was to be placed outstretched on the wheel; their limbs held over the gaps in the spokes. A hammer would then be mounted above the wheel, and as the wheel turned, it would strike the victim in each of its limbs, crushing them with each blow. If the victim was fortunate enough, the hammer would strike his chest, crushing it and causing instant death. The unlucky ones would suffer agonizing pain until their bodies gave out.

The brazen bull was a new torture device Vlad was anxious to try. It was a large, hollow bull made of bronze. It had a door large enough for a man to fit through, and that latched on the outside. It was situated over a fire pit. The victim would be placed inside the bull and a fire would be lit underneath the bull, burning the victim alive inside with no possibility of escape. Vlad mentally drooled at the anticipation of hearing the noblemen scream for their lives as they cooked to death.

Vlad's final request for his second wish was the blood extractor. He wished he had saved one more prisoner from the battle to test all three of these devices. Maybe he would spare one of the noblemen the other two devices so he could concentrate on the mechanics of the extractor. It was an experimental tool that mortuary members used to extract the blood of the deceased before they were nailed into their coffins. He was most curious about this device.

Vlad swept his hands in front of the two nobles and bowed. "Welcome to my humble chamber, dear sirs," his venomous words spewed from his mouth. The stone chamber, with its crude dirt floor, reeked of mildew and dead vermin. Tiny skeletons crunched under the feet of the men entering the chamber. Oh, how he savored this moment. These men who had made him grovel in shame were now his to do whatever his sadistic heart wanted. Vlad remembered their laughing when he had presented his gifts in hopes of getting the votes he needed for his father's vacated position. The man he pointed to first had been the one mocking him the most.

"Why don't I start with you, Freng?" Vlad stepped over to the man quivering in his boots. "You had hoped I wouldn't recognize you, huh?" He sliced through the ropes still tied at his wrists. Grabbing Freng by his hair, he dragged him to the brazen bull. Vlad's eyes flashed with a vengeance. Genie ached inside for the man. Again, he wanted nothing to do with what he was about to witness.

Vlad shoved Freng into the open side of the brazen bull but not without sustaining several kicks and attempted blows from the reluctant victim. He seemed to pay the floundering man no attention as his resistance only intensified Vlad's resolve. Once inside, he slammed the door shut and pushed the latch in place, sealing Freng's doom.

"So, you thought it funny to mock me when I humbly stood before you, asking for what was rightfully mine, eh?" Vlad hissed. "Well, you won't find any humor in there."

Lup, the second nobleman, stood in utter shock and disbelief as he could only watch what was happening before him. He soiled his pants as he watched Vlad bring the fire to life from under the brazen bull. Slowly, the flames began to lick the underside of the bronze coffin. The flames grew higher as the screams inside grew louder. Freng could be heard, through the shrieks of pain, hopelessly kicking the metal sides of the bull. The smell of burning flesh permeated the room. Vlad stood beside the bronze beast with his arms folded across his chest as if bored by the ordeal. His only movement was when he inhaled the smell of his victim's frying body. Then, for what seemed like an eternity, the screams and kicks finally faded and eventually stopped. Vlad did not bother himself by freeing the burnt corpse inside, he spun on his heels and faced Lup.

Too shocked to have tried to move while Freng roasted to death, Lup suddenly realized he was next to be tortured. Survival instinct took hold of him, and he ran towards the door to escape. Vlad's evil laugh echoed in the stone chamber as he grabbed the rope still attached to Lup. He yanked the rope, sending Lup backward, and he landed on his back on the floor from the force of the tug.

Vlad stood over the man, straddling him on either side of his torso. "So, you too think I am nothing in this village. I am the lowest of all peasants in your eyes, eh?"

"No, no, not at all!" he frantically pleaded. "I was the only one who thought you should take your father's place. It was Freng and the others who didn't find you fit to govern. I... I...it was I that stood up for you." Lup grasped at any possible words to satisfy Vlad, to make him understand that he was innocent of the crimes Vlad was accusing him of.

"You lie," he sneered. "The whole of the noblemen saw me useless, an annoying thorn in their arrogant sides. You included. I heard nothing from you in my defense."

He grabbed Lup's shirt and hoisted him to his feet. With Lup in his firm grasp, he hastily strode to the table on the chamber's far wall. He slammed Lup down on a wooden table and secured his limbs to it with the leather straps attached to the sides of the table. Lup was still able to wiggle his body and tried to break from his confinements. It was no use. The straps were too new and firm. They held his arms and legs firmly in place.

Vlad retrieved the last of diabolical requests. The blood extractor. The simple device consisted of a hollow metal stick-like instrument. It had been shaved to a point but only on one side, leaving an oval hole at the top. Its purpose was to be stuck into a corpse's lifeless jugular vein so any trapped blood inside the body would drain from it. Vlad had no intention of draining Lup's blood. He intended to drink it. Killing Lup before he inserted the extractor would not serve his purpose. He wanted the blood warm. He wanted it to flow into his mouth with each pulse of his heartbeat.

Genie floated above, too paralyzed to offer the poor nobleman any help. There was no window for him to escape, even temporarily through. He was trapped; forced to observe Vlad while he carried out this ghastly deed. He watched him shove the metal object deep into Lup's neck. Blood immediately flowed through the tube with such a force that the reddish liquid arced over the table to the floor, pulsing as the precious life substance drained from the man.

When the stream slowed just a bit, Genie turned in disgust as he saw Vlad lock his mouth over the metal tube and drink the blood of his prisoner. He drank and drank until the pulsing stopped. Only then did he slump on the floor and pass out.

The silence tormented Genie worse than all the screaming. Two men lay dead, and one lay in repulsive satisfaction. Genie's stomach churned at the sight before him. He could still smell the acid of Lup's blood and the burning of Freng's flesh. Sunrise would be soon, and he prayed Vlad would slumber past its arrival. Then Genie would not have to grant another wish. He would return to his lamp. What happened after that, he did not care, he wanted to be gone from this place. From this man. He floated towards a narrow window braced with three metal posts.

*How easily I could slip away*, he thought.

His silent plea would not be answered. He wistfully watched Vlad stir and rise from his all-too-brief slumber. Groggy from his escapades of battle, the exhilaration of the killing, and the indescribable pleasure from consuming Lup's blood. He rubbed his eyes and wiped his mouth. He stared down at the smear of blood on his hands and smiled. He felt such power surge through him, invigorating him. Never before had he felt so alive! It was as if he was born again. He felt virile. Youthful. Immortal. It had to be from the blood. This newfound energy had to be from the blood!  He wanted more. He jumped to his feet and anxiously started pacing the floor, observing the carnage he had created.

Glancing back and forth to his lifeless victims, he thought about using his last wish to ask for more prisoners to be brought to him so he could achieve this resurgence he felt from drinking Lup's blood again. But a different thought struck him. What if he drank the blood of a diseased man? Would he, too, be tainted? No. He had to think, and he had to think fast. He frantically remembered that he only had until sunrise to make his final wish.

Genie watched as Vlad contemplated his next wish. His eerie silence made Genie nervous. He couldn't read his thoughts nor gauge his emotions as he paced the room, as if in a trance. His body may not have been indicating his thoughts, but Vlad's mind was twirling with ideas.

*Sure, I could always find prisoners to take in or even the peasants begging for coin throughout the countryside*, he thought. *Would younger blood taste better than that of elderly one? How can I entice a young innocent to come to me?*

He would have to become charming, a trait he currently lacked.

The quietude continued as Vlad stopped and stared motionless at the wall. Suddenly, he snapped his head up to Genie. "I have my last wish," he whispered into the air.

Genie was relieved that this would be his last wish to be granted, and he could be rid of this horrid place. He was not expecting what he heard for Vlad's final wish.

"I wish to live in the silence of the night. I no longer desire the warmth of sunshine on my face. No more do I want to fight battles or bow to noblemen. I'm tired of trying to fulfill my father's destiny that was taken from him." He almost serenaded the wish from his lips. He spoke with such passion and desire, almost as if the night would become his loving mistress.

Genie could not believe what he was hearing. He had thought for sure Vlad would use his final wish for vile purposes. Had he misread the man's lust for torture? Had something changed in the man that he had missed seeing? As he listened to the rest of Vlad's words, he realized he had missed something, and it was worse than he had anticipated.

"I want to be left alone, with two caveats," Vlad continued. "I want to be able to roam undetectable as a man when I venture out at night, and I no longer want to live on the sustenance of the land; I want to feast on the blood of my enemies." Vlad watched as Genie listened to his words. He could see his eyes struck by the repulsive request. Vlad cared nothing about what the Wishkeeper thought of him; he only desired a way that he could forever feel the euphoria he felt when he drank Lup's blood. The idea consumed his every fiber.

"I grant you your wish," Genie said in languished defeat. He had truly wanted the man before him to have found some sense of humility, some sense of decency. It was apparent that he was sorely mistaken. Before the wish commenced, he needed to find a way to curb Vlad's bloodlust—a way that could potentially destroy him in the future.

Genie was still learning his powers, so he wasn't sure what he could do. He impulsively set his caveat.

Unbeknownst to Vlad, Genie placed upon him a weakness that would render him defenseless against drawing the blood from his victims. If his victims wore a cross necklace or held one in their hands, Vlad could not touch them. His experience with the man in Golgotha, the one Pilate had crucified, had shown through the trace memories of Vlad and the stories told down through the centuries since, an unexplainable power of peace and love. Those who followed him long after his death had revered him and worshiped him. Artifacts of their loyalty to this man included many adaptations of the very object he had been slain upon. A cross. That simple object would be Vlad's downfall. Genie begged silently for the powers that made him - *let it work*.

# 9
# GENIE'S DAMNATION

Once again, Genie found himself back in his lamp. What had initially been a perceived prison now felt like a paradise in comparison to the outside world. He did not know how long it would be until he was summoned to servitude again, but for now, he could find some peace. He just wanted to be as far from Vlad as possible. Maybe he and his lamp would be taken from the abominable place of Vlad's homeland. Somewhere, or some time, where men like Vlad didn't exist anymore.

Genie sat with his thoughts for a lengthy amount of time. He reflected on what had recently transpired. He began to draw similarities between Vlad and Titus. These two men were so alike it was frightening.

*Could it be that they carried some innate demonic trait?* He wondered. *Was it a deformity in their minds that made them do these horrendous acts upon their fellow human beings? Could it be the time in which they had been born? Do I still carry parallel attributions?*

Oh, how he hoped not, but his internal struggle surfaced.

If he had to be honest with himself, a part of him was still partial to the cruelty he witnessed deep down in the recesses of his existence. He didn't want to admit this, not even to himself. Their actions kindled the flames he thought he had fought hard to extinguish. Though he was truly repulsed by the savagery and ferociousness of the gore, he felt himself wanting to be Titus or Vlad. Wanting to participate in their acts of torture. It sickened him to feel this way, even in the tiniest slivers of his soul, but the thoughts lingered. He did not want to be either of those men. He did not want to feel any ounce of pleasure from their malevolence.

*Maybe*, he thought, *this was my curse.*

Perhaps, until he was able to break free from his greed and bloodthirstiness, he would continue to be condemned to carry out the bidding of evil men. If he could just rid himself of these essences of thoughts that couldn't be passed onto the orb, he could deal with this life he had been fated to.

An idea struck him. Maybe it wasn't him after all. Maybe the lamp in which he was confined made him harbor these thoughts. He had heard of evil spirits haunting the buildings in his hometown when he had been Hasba. Could it be that the lamp itself was cursed since he was found in an area known for its superstitions? If that were true, all he had to do was destroy the lamp the next time he was freed from its boundary. A colossal task, no doubt, but could it be possible, he contemplated.

It wouldn't be long before Genie could test his theory. Once again, he felt himself pulled through the lamp and out into the world. He could tell immediately that he was no longer in Romania. This place was vibrant and abuzz with something Genie could not quite grasp. There was fervent in the air, like a purpose of a reality that needed to come to fruition.

# 10
# TOMÁS

The man that called up and now stood before Genie was bald, save for a ring of hair that encircled his head. He was a rather stout, frumpy man covered head to toe in a heavy black robe with clasps unfamiliar to Genie. Around his neck hung a chain with a bulky cross attached to it. Upon seeing the cross, Genie's spirits lifted. Here was a man who followed the one from Titus' time! This man before him could not be as deviant as Titus and Vlad. Or so he had thought. The man stood frozen in trepidation at the wispy deity floating before his confused and frightened eyes.

To verify time again, Genie reached out to touch the man's forehead. He at first jerked away from the advance of this spirit, but when Genie touched him, he felt comforted and leaned into the pressure.

*This must be a sign from God that I am being tested in my faith*, he mused.

Genie realized at once he had been mistaken in thinking this man had any benevolence inside his soul. His lack of compassion was apparent as soon as Genie pierced his memories. This man had the same twisted trait as his previous two Masters. He didn't want to learn more about this man, but he needed to figure out his surroundings. The land around him was strange; filled with greenery and flowers the likes he had never seen. The aromatic smells permeated the air with their sweet fragrances. The scents soothed him, but he quickly remembered the task at hand. Though it nauseated him, he delved further into the man's thoughts.

Times and places were a little easier to ascertain now. The man's thoughts showed that he was in a country called Spain. The time was 1479. It was a time of great religious upheaval and division. The man Genie had seen suffering upon the very cross symbolized on the necklace around this man so long ago and saw how his followers only brought peace, had now been betrayed. Or, rather, his teachings had. So many had used his name for ill-gotten purposes. The man before him was one of them.

"I am the genie of the Lamp," Genie, now for a third time was forced to grant another sadist his wishes. He finished reciting the rules to this man.

"I am called Tomás," the man uttered. He looked at this mystical being with suspicion. He still wasn't convinced of his holy test. "What sorcery are you?"

"I am no sorcerer. I am a genie. I bring you a chance for three wishes to fulfill your life, a chance to bring to fruition whatever you desire. What will you wish for?" Genie spread his hands wide to show he meant no harm.

"You are a detestable creature of Satan! How dare you approach me." The solace he had felt before dissipated into fear and trepidation. Tomás considered himself a supreme holy man and this vile apparition before him was everything he stood against. God had sent a demon to test his faith!

"You will not tempt me! I will not give in to your allurement! Do you think I am some kind of fool that I would succumb to you and your traps of gratification?" he spat at Genie.

"Ah, so you think that I can force you to wish for that which goes against your purity?" Genie asked with genuine curiosity. "I cannot make you want something that you don't. Your wishes come from you, from inside your soul, from your thoughts, from your desires. Not mine. You could even wish for my freedom if you so wanted." A spark of hope flashed in Genie as he explained this.

"Why would I wish for your freedom? I do not desire to have you walk this earth untethered!"

Genie could see that he could say nothing to make this man understand the power he could behold, even if for a short time. Genie was also unsure what to do should this man not wish for anything. Divine-Genie did not cover this scenario. Would he be doomed to follow this man throughout his mortal life, lying in wait for him to wish for something? Maybe that's exactly what he would have to do.

Tomás began walking towards the middle of town, carrying the lamp. He had business to attend to and would not be stopped by the devil's demon. He decided to ignore the blue mist following him, though his thoughts started down the path of the temptation he sought to ignore. He had just been granted the position of Grand Inquisitor. A position he had longed for to help his country rid itself of the miscreants that currently inhabited it. He had been granted the authority to purge Spain of anyone who dared deviate from its current state of cleansing. He had the ultimate say on how to accomplish this vast task. Having this genie, as it called itself, grant him certain liberties to achieve this goal, especially if it could be done quickly, would elevate his appeal to the Pope. An achievement he most desired.

Finally, red-faced and sweating, he reached his destination—a small church located directly in the middle of all the hustle and bustle of its residents. Tomás walked through the thick wooden doors, shutting them behind him and preventing the genie from entering the sanctuary. Tomás was dismayed as he watched the apparition mystically appear inside.

"Get out!" he screamed at Genie. Several friars were milling about inside the church. Some were in silent prayer, while others were in hushed discussions. Upon hearing the loud, sudden outburst, they rushed to their brother.

"Tomás, what has taken over you?" They stood around Tomás. Their brows furrowed with sincere concern. Tomás looked around at his fellow brothers in faith. Their worried frowns gave him no inclination that they were aware of the ghastly being floating in the vestibule. This caused him some concern. They could not see this genie. He wondered if the genie's touch had scrambled his mind. He had heard of those who had delusions and the treatments for such cases. He did not want to be thought of as contracting this ailment.

Trying to quell his anger at the genie and distract his brothers from further questions, he mumbled some reassuring words about being tired and needing sleep under his breath. He brushed past them and headed for his dorm. His solitude. A place where he would not be disturbed further, as the brothers dared not follow the Grand Inquisitor into his private sanctuary. Genie, again, drifted into the room even as Tomás slammed the door behind him.

"Will you never leave me?" Tomás exasperatedly inquired.

"I cannot leave until your three wishes are granted or until you set me free of your own accord," Genie repeated.

"Very well," Tomás quipped. "Since you have given me no other options, I will issue to you my first wish, if only to be rid of your sordid self!"

Genie folded his arms in anticipation of the forthcoming wish. He watched as Tomás placed the lamp on a small table beside a crude bed. He hoped he could find some time to test his theory on its destruction. However, he hadn't figured it all out, especially the part where if he destroyed the lamp while he was released, what would happen to him. He surely didn't want to live out the rest of his days in this form. The more he battled the possibility of forced freedom, the more he realized it was not going to be. He was too afraid of the consequences of destroying the lamp. He half-heartedly listened to his new master demand his first wish.

<h1 style="text-align:center">11</h1>

# TOMÁS' LUST

"**A**s you know, I am the Grand Inquisitor of Spain," Tomás began touting his accomplishment. So confident was he that he couldn't care less whether this genie knew of his Grand Inquisitor title. In his arrogance, he assumed everyone would know who and what he was by his stature and dress.

"My duties include ridding this country of its heathens and non-followers of the true and rightful faith. This is a very daunting task that has been asked of me and I intend to flourish in its undertaking. I need a way to differentiate the heathens from true men of faith. They practice their rituals in secrecy so as not to be discovered. I wish to have a patch of cloth placed upon the clothes of those who are not true believers. The cloth must depict an insignia that contrasts with the symbols of my faith."

Genie obediently nodded his head. "Your wish has been granted." Although he disagreed about separating those of a certain faith from their homeland, Genie surmised that the wish was not as devastating as he had seen.

In his mortal life as a youth, there were plenty of people that townspeople avoided or even ostracized. Little did he know, but he would eventually discover that this branding would cause tens of thousands of people to be banished from the country with only what possessions they could carry. A patch with a star surrounded by a circle appeared instantly on thousands of people throughout the country. They stared in confusion at the appearance of this unwanted addition to their garb.

Tomás sat on his cot for some time without speaking. He was deep in thought. How would he know if what he had wished for really took place? He could leave his room and check the town to verify his request. It was full of unbelievers. He worried, though, that the brothers might again think him hysterical if they saw him running around the town inspecting the clothing of passers-by. He did not want that assumption associated with him at this precarious time.

He decided to stay put and mull over his next wish. He would follow through with this insanity of wishes. Anything to get rid of the genie. His mere presence caused him great strife. However, as much as he despised the notion, he wasn't ready to give up this chance to make a name for himself. Not only did he need to expel the wicked, but he also needed to be certain that those who remained were loyal to the faith. As Grand Inquisitor, he would make sure that only the purest remained, pure men of faith, and when the Pope visited, which he was apt to do unannounced, he would see how the country rallied to his Papal cause.

Tomás thought back to his childhood. He had held a deep-seeded hatred for women that stemmed from an early age. His mother, a useless whore in his mind, was the catalyst of this loathing. He had tried repeatedly to please her in his youthful ways. It made no difference to him. His mere existence maddened her. She would frequently beat him for the slightest infraction in her eyes all because he reminded her of his father. A scoundrel who had promised to marry her after he had his way with her, but as it turned out, he was already married. To his whore-mongering father, she was just a passing fancy for his wanderlust. His mother begged him to reconsider or at least help her financially. She had been a stupid, lustful woman in Tomás' eyes. No matter how menial, no one would give her employment with a bastard in tow. The only choice his mother had was to enter a convent. It was within the walls of the convent that he developed his faith and love for the church. It was his only solace; however, he suffered abuse from the nuns who took turns with him when he reached manhood.

The nuns would sneak into his room late at night when the brothers were asleep or in their rooms, flogging themselves in an obscene attempt to purify their thoughts and desires. The nuns had no stomach for such self-inflicted abuse. They would rub themselves along Tomás' woolen robes until they felt his stiffness grow. Hitching up their robes, they would mount and ride him until their pleasures were released, leaving Tomás feeling unsatisfied and disgusted as they creeped out of his room. Many times, he would have to expel his wonton pleasure with his hand. He tried in vain to distract their advances by gorging himself at every opportunity, thinking his fatness would deter their lust. It didn't and his plump figure was all he had to show for his efforts.

Disengaging from those lustful thoughts of his youth, Tomás turned to Genie. "I want all the women in the surrounding houses to gather in the square. In the center of the square, I want a burning stake mounted. This is my second wish." He thought this would be his revenge for all the anguish the nuns had caused him.

Puzzled at the request, Genie could only say, "I grant you your wish." Tomás leaped from his bed and ran out of the room, through the hallway, and out the great door into the town streets. His fellow faithful could only stare agape at his hurried departure. He ran to the center of town, where about fifty bewildered women stood huddled together, trying to understand how and why they were there. Genie was momentarily left alone with the lamp after Tomás' departure. He toyed with destroying it again before an unspoken force compelled him to follow his master.

One by one, Tomás questioned the women gathered in the square. Even if they wore no star, he cast the ones he deemed heretical to the other side of the ones he still interrogated. Some women answered his questions in a manner he felt appropriate, and they were told to leave. Afraid to stay a second longer, they rushed back to their homes. Very few women were granted this clemency. The remaining women grew even more fearful as they watched their friends be allowed to leave.

Tomás instilled the help of some of the town folks who had heard the commotion to tie the women's hands. Tomás appealed to them by explaining that these women were heretics. He had questioned them and found them to have practiced witchcraft, which was strictly against religious law. The women cried in protest but were ignored as the men listened to Tomás' fervent tirade against them.

Tomás grabbed the nearest woman. She was in her mid-twenties. An appealing maiden with long blonde hair and the bluest eyes. Her bosoms were still swollen from having recently given birth. She pleaded with Tomás as she tried to pull away from him. He tightened his grip as he dragged her across the square to the burning stake. Shaking in fear and horror, she could only scream.

"What have I done wrong, good sir?" Her frantic pleas as they fell on Tomás' enraged deaf ears.

He had picked this one first because she had looked so much like his mother. He curled his lips in a vicious snarl as he tied her to the stake. Caught up in the passion of what was happening before them, the townsfolk started to chant in encouragement.

"Burn her! Burn her! Burn the witch!" They repeated as they watched Tomás light the fire at the feet of the innocent woman. The other women stared in disbelief at the event unfolding before them. The reality of the situation set in, and they tried to escape. They were not swift enough and the blood-thirsty men grabbed them before they took three steps towards freedom.

Genie watched again in revulsion as Tomás carried out his gruesome mission. These women represented the manifestation of the hatred he had for his mother. It was his revenge upon those who made him have ill thoughts and desires that did not align with his faith. The faith he felt was his true calling.

Every woman Tomás declared an unbeliever, burned in the square one by one. Smoke and ash thickened the air around the square. The fevered crowd started to gag at the noxious fumes. The smell of charred skin hung in the air as the screams died out. The cheers, too, had faded, and the men left him. The last hostage had fainted from shock before she too, was hauled to the stake and scorched. Leaving Tomás alone to observe his triumph, he watched her squirm and scream as she slowly burned.

"I still have one more wish, you devil," he said as he pulled his gaze from the flames and turned to the Genie. "Take me to my mother's grave and open it." At once, Genie and Tomás were standing at the foot of an open grave. A hole had been dug exposing its contents below. The stench of decay hung in the air. Tomás jumped into the unearthed hole and pulled the lid back from the coffin. He stared at the figure inside, its darkened skin peeling back from bones. Tomás' mother stared with hollow sockets at her son, baring her teeth with an eerie smile.

"You did this to me," he grunted at the corpse. "You put these unholy thoughts in my head. You sowed a demon seed inside me that I did not ask for. I was just a boy! I wanted your love and all you gave me was misery. But look at me now, Mother! I have power. I have fame. I will soon have fortune when the Holy Father sees how I have rid this place of people like you!" Tomás screamed at the silent bones. He hoisted his shoulders back and puffed his chest in superiority to the long-dead figure below. Hitching up his robes, he uncovered his manhood and caddishly urinated on his mother's remains.

Lowering his robe once he had finished, he turned his back to his mother and drew himself up from the grave. Looking around for the genie, he spotted the lamp. His third wish had been granted. Genie was gone. He quickly picked up the lamp and threw it into the open earth. It landed with a thud in his mother's coffin. Tomás scooped the dirt around the grave with his hands, throwing it back into the hole until it had been filled again.

No one would ever find Genie again, *or so he thought.*

# 12
# GENIE'S CONFLICT

**"I** cannot tolerate this any longer!" Genie screamed into the emptiness of his confinement. After granting Tomás' wishes, he found himself, once again, alone, and back in his prison. He wanted to vomit, but his stomach contained no substance that he could eliminate. *Three!* Three vile men had succeeded in their cravings for evil, and he was to blame for giving it to them. He stomped around the room shaking his fists at the nothingness. If he could have drunk himself into a stupor to forget everything he'd gladly partake in many fiery beverages.

The only remedy was to extract the memories and lock them in the memory orb—a small condolence of his tormented mind. With an unsteady hand, he pulled the memories from their entrapment and released them from his thoughts. A dull trace of their existence still lingered, however. Their echoes would forever remain a part of him. It was a condition of his curse—to forever taste if ever so slightly, the wickedness of his wish consumers.

What haunted him was his connection to these vile men. He must still possess deviant traits for there was a small part of him that reveled in their torture and lust. It was as if he was a part of their acts. Some fraction of his soul connected to them, and he hated himself.

*If ever granted mortality, would I carry this abhorred conscience into that life? Would I seek to inflict the same torment upon innocent humanity?* These thoughts plagued him.

The better part of him wanted nothing to do with that life, yet the evilness twirled quietly inside him.

Time stood still, or at least that's what it felt like, as Genie contemplated all this. Flashes of greed, lust, torture, and pain flew through his psyche. His dreams tormented him with visions of cardinal longings. He cried out many times to Morpheus to quiet his slumber. His waking hours also haunted him with the etches of his Wishkeeper demands.

He tussled with his immortality as well.

*What would happen to me if I never was able to gain my freedom? Would I, too, become like Divine-Genie? Would I gain the power to create more genies? Would I renounce the need to rid myself of disgustful desires and give in to them? Would I exist until the end of time? Were there even a thousand opportunities for wishes to be granted? What if I and my lamp were never to be found again?*

He would soon discover that his lamp was more sought after than anticipated.

Unbeknownst to him, the hole that Tomás had so compactly filled had finally been uncovered by grave robbers in search of treasure. It did not take them long to discover the lavish lamp buried deep beneath the Earth. The stench of the dead did not keep them from their cache of jewels and discarded fortune. The loot was to be sold for gold or silver to the many brokers of such fine artifacts. The merchants cared not from where their bounty came. From then on, Genie's lamp changed through many hands, untouched by skin that could have unleashed him and his powers. The lamp traveled far and wide until it found its way to Hungary. The lamp would be part of a dowry given to a woman named Elizabeth.

# 13

# ELIZABETH

Elizabeth fumbled through her wooden dowry chest. The ornate box smelled of stuffy cloth and cedar. She was furiously looking for anything of value. It had been a few years since she had looked upon it. She did not need it as her wealthy husband provided well for her. Her husband was a well-to-do nobleman, a Count, nonetheless, and she did not need the riches the chest contained. Until now. Her beloved, Count Ferenc, had been called to war, and a lone female was a prime target for looters and those looking for trouble while the men were away in far-off lands. Hoping the contents of her dowry chest would appease these opportunistic men, she emptied the contents in search of bribe offerings. The thieves had come knocking, scoping the castle which she called home. Her servants had shooed them away, but they would soon be back.

She hated being in this predicament. She didn't know what to do. She never felt so alone. She had always been coddled by her father and had been his favorite child. Her sister developed a deep animosity towards her by the time Elizabeth was three years old. Her father's eyes would light up any time Elizabeth entered the room, any time she showed him her embroidery, any time she showed him a new dress that was made for her. Elizabeth's father doted on her. Her sister, on the other hand, tried in vain to capture their father's attention. Her father would simply wave her off as if she were a bother anytime she would show him her skills or a new wardrobe.

Elizabeth didn't see the joy her father bestowed upon her. She only saw her sister constantly vying for their father's attention. Rather than be satisfied with the abundance of attention her father gave, she silently seethed at her sister's deliberate attempts to sway their father's love. Elizabeth did not take well to any woman who innocently tried to grab the attention of the men in her life, including her husband.

She saw the way the maidens tried to throw themselves at her husband when they were in court. Even the queen would smile a little too long when her husband had presented her to their Majesties. Elizabeth developed an unhealthy jealousy towards women. Her husband would chastise her when they had returned home, accusing her of making a fool of herself in front of all the nobility. Elizabeth brushed off his accusations by appeasing his sexual appetite in their bed. Deep down, though, she harbored rage as she rode him until he released himself inside her. He mistook her animalistic lovemaking as a reconciliation for her inexcusable outbursts.

Temporarily repressing those memories, she returned to her inspection. The chest contained the usual contents of a dowry: fine linens, silk dresses, water jugs, and candlesticks made of the finest silver, rings, and necklaces adorned with precious jewels, and one single object carefully wrapped in deep blue velvet. She smiled at the sack. A single blue item in a sea of white fabric and dull metal caught her eye. Blue was her favorite color. The entire chest had been given to her by her husband, a practice unheard of in those times, as a wedding gift. Her husband was of a lower nobility than her father was at the time, so it was he who provided the necessary token of his love and to prove to her father that he could provide for her once they were married. Her father reluctantly agreed, but Elizabeth swore her undying love for the simple, handsome man. Her husband later made a substantial name for himself, calming all her father's fears.

Carefully unrolling the velvet cloth, feeling its soft texture as it slid through her hands, Elizabeth uncovered the luxurious lamp. She puzzled over the object, turning it over in her hands, admiring its beauty but also intrigued by its uniqueness. She wondered where her husband had found such a gem of a trinket. She hesitated her inspection when she noticed a smudge in the finish. She rubbed the velvet cloth over the distortion hoping to bring it back to shine. The cloth did nothing to remove the blemish. Licking the palm of her hand, she worked at the spot.

She threw the lamp from her as it started to vibrate and warm. Genie emerged from the lamp. Scrambling backward across the room, she hurriedly slammed into the wall to escape the all-but-transparent milky figure before her. Accustomed to the reaction, Genie swirled above her without comment until he realized this was not a man but a woman who had released him.

"You are a woman!" Genie exclaimed in astonishment. He did not expect to see a female. Everyone before had all been men.

*Men*, he thought, *had the violent genes, surely not an attribute of the softer gender.*

A glimmer of optimism poured over him.

*Surely, the fair maiden before me would not harbor evil thoughts. Or, could this be my chance to finally be free?*

Bright-eyed and still fearful, Elizabeth pointed at Genie. Her thoughts projected what her mouth could not speak. Genie composed himself and softly explained who he was and what powers he possessed. Elizabeth's breath slowly returned to a normal rate, but she was still shocked at what her eyes could not erase no matter how many times she blinked them.

Genie patiently waited while she absorbed all he had spoken. She silently repeated the rules outlined: three wishes: before the sunset, this ghostly being could not kill anyone, and she could not make someone fall in love with her. That one rule stuck with her a little longer.

*Why would I want anyone to fall in love with me? I love my husband. I want my husband to be in love with me.*

Elizabeth's thoughts started to veer drastically from the fascination of finding the lamp to thoughts of her husband's imagined infidelity. She started to wonder if her husband was in love with someone else. Her mind raced with images of her husband bedding women he encountered through the towns after each battle. Maybe this gift wasn't a trinket of devotion after all. Maybe it was meant to be found and he had known all along what power it possessed. It was a vehicle to have her deemed hysterical and, therefore, put away so he could marry someone else, someone younger.

She continued this vein of thought for some time. It started to consume her thoughts. Jealousy crept into her being. She became agitated at the notion of her husband's unfaithfulness. Genie watched as Elizabeth slipped into an enraged state of mind. He saw her eyes flicker quickly back and forth as the silent war raged inside her thoughts. He shrugged in despair knowing what was forthcoming. He could almost predict an unpleasant outcome of his magical generosity but was still hopeful for a pleasant request. Her eyes pierced Genie as she made her first wish. Her repressed jealousy bolted to the surface of her consciousness.

"Have all the maidens in the area come to me. I will teach them the art of embroidery. A skill they must learn if they are to become noblewomen and have the chance for a proper marriage into society." Elizabeth smiled at her cunningness. The skillfully crafted lie slipped smoothly from her lips so that Genie could not detect the slightest hint of deception. Perplexed by the command, Genie had no recourse but to grant her wish.

He would soon find out exactly what she intended.

# 14

# ELIZABETH'S DELUSION

O ne by one, the young women around the village came to the grand mansion. Unaware of why they found themselves with such an urge to travel to the mansion, they stood in awe at the gates, looking around at the expanse of grounds. Everything surrounding them was perfect. The topiary was sculpted into whimsical shapes of nymphs, birds, and even an elephant. Tiny white pebbles formed vast pathways around the gardens. The mansion itself stood majestically before them, springing with thoughts of themselves living in such luxury. Their confusion shifted to wonderment.

Elizabeth greeted each with warm hugs and smiles, encouraging them to wander about the place and take in all they could see. She desperately wanted them to come inside, but she bid her time as they gaped and awed. She even heard giggling as clusters of girls ran through the maze of flowerbeds and carefully placed bronze gnomes.

Genie, unseen by the girls, was pleased to see such lightheartedness. He had been wallowing in despair for too long from all he had witnessed before. The joy and laughter in the air made his heart sing with delight. He had almost burst out in song but held himself in check and simply admired the scene before him.

After the girls had had their fill of the landscape, they made their way into the mansion. The wonder they found outside was overshadowed by what they observed inside. The sheer grandeur of the countess' residence took their breath away. They stood with gaping mouths and wide eyes as they swirled around looking at the contents inside.

The walls were adorned with lush tapestries from lands they had only heard of from their fathers' tales of faraway places. Paintings were hung depicting lords and ladies of the past. People, they assumed, were the ancestors of the count and countess. Men and women were forever captured in art, never to be forgotten as their unwavering eyes peered over the domain they once inhabited.

"Come. Come, my darlings," the countess sweetly beckoned, breaking the girls' enthrallment of their surroundings, and ushered them into the vast dining hall.

The elaborate, long table had been assembled in all its splendor, and each girl was placed around it in chairs upholstered in soft, cushion-like fabric. One by one, they took their seats. Never before had they seen such finery. Delicate bone China plates, one slightly larger than the other sat stacked in front of their chair. Shiny cutlery was placed on either side of the plates. Crystal clear glasses stood waiting to be filled with the choicest wines. Elegant linens waiting to be unfolded onto the laps of its guests were folded into triangle shapes and placed with precision atop the plates.

Before entering the room, Elizabeth stole herself to a corner of the grand foyer and whispered for Genie to follow her. She did not want to appear to be talking to herself by the girls.

"I have decided on my last two wishes. One, I will tell you now. The other must wait until later."

Genie listened intently as she made her request. He reminded her that her three wishes must be requested before sunset. Waving his boring required speech away with her hand, she made her second wish.

"Go upstairs to my room and place a dozen chairs around the fireplace. Light the fireplace, too. I want the room to be warm for my guests," she commanded. Genie listened as he watched Elizabeth carefully form her words.

He could touch her forehead to understand her motivations, but he hesitated. He deeply desired her wishes to be for good. She seemed so innocent and pure. Surely, no harm would come to the jovial girls in the other room. Or so he hoped.

"At each chair," Elizabeth continued, "place an assortment of colored thread, embroidery needles, and a patch of white sewing cloth."

Her request seemed harmless, giving Genie a feeling of relief. *There was good inside this woman*, he thought.

Genie furrowed his eyebrows. He was perplexed by this command. Could he have become so suspicious that even the smallest, benign request had caused him doubt? He toiled over her reasoning for this wish. He could not think of any malicious harm she could cause with what she had asked for. Oh, how naïve he was.

Elizabeth returned to her guests as Genie glided upstairs to do her bidding, but not before she made a quick stop at an ornate mahogany cabinet. On the top shelf, a hidden bottle of sleeping juice was wedged into the dark corner of the cupboard. Looking around to make sure she was alone; she hastily hid the bottle in a secret pocket sewn into the folds of her dress. Smoothing out any wrinkles, she entered the room, full of smiles and welcoming words. She transformed into the most gracious host.

Two-by-two, servants entered the room carrying trays of the most tantalizing food the girls had ever seen. Each servant walked on either side of the table, filling each plate with rich, delicious food. Wide-eyed, the maidens stared in wonderment as the servants dished out succulent pork and mutton, heaps of potatoes and vegetables, and berries onto their plates. The girls could only gaze in awe at the feast before them. Bellies began to rumble as the scent of the food drifted to their noses. Impatient to eat but not wanting to appear ungracious, they sat with their hands in their laps.

"Welcome, each of you!" Elizabeth greeted her audience. "I know you are wondering why I have called you here today. And I will tell you in due time, I assure you. But, first, let us eat. You must all be hungry, yes?" Each girl nodded in agreement, still hesitant at what was expected of them. Some girls were brave enough to grab pieces of meat and start chewing on the deliciousness. Others were more reserved as if waiting for permission. A few were even afraid to touch the meal for fear it would vanish before their eyes.

"Wait!" Elizabeth blurted, catching some of the girls in mid-chew. "I forgot your wine. How silly of me."

At their mistress' command, the servants poured a deep, burgundy wine into each of the glasses. The girls could not contain their excitement. They were not allowed to indulge in such fineries at home.

"Now, before you drink this wine, I must warn you, it is a tad bitter. It comes from a very dry region in a country called Gaul. The grapes, from which wine is made if you did not know, grow high on the hilltops so they are closer to the sun, making their taste a little tart, especially for ladies. I have with me drops that will help lessen the bitterness, making it taste a little sweeter. If you permit me, I will put one tiny, little drop in each of your glasses."  The girls nodded in unison, too excited to taste the wine to question the countess' false tale.

Elizabeth unfolded the bottle hidden in her skirt and began infusing their drinks with a small drop of sleeping juice. With each droplet, she let out a mischievous chortle.

"Now, eat!" she proclaimed and sat down to join in the abundant meal. She watched the girls devour their food and wash it all down with the wine, watching with glee as they began to fill their mouths.

While the girls ate, Elizabeth remarked on why they were there.

"I brought you here today to teach you the art of embroidery. Now, now, before you protest," she held her hand up to stop the hushed sighs of displeasure coming from the enchanted wards. "Embroidery is a skill that each of you should learn before you are married. It is expected of young women to know this artform. It is an art; I can tell you. It took me many years to master it. The women of your new families will require you to sit with them and embroider your dresses or scarves with intricate scenes of your husband's family history."

"Do we ever tell *our* family history in our sewing, Countess?" one inquisitive girl asked.

"Oh, no, my dear sweet child," Elizabeth countered. "Your duty, once married, is to your husband and his family. You cannot assert your own feelings or wants. That would cause your husband grief and it may also cause him to wander to another's bed." Jealousy crept into her words. Pushing down the emotion that threatened her ploy, she continued.

"What I mean to say is that your husband and his family will be pleased with your efforts to enshrine their existence, and you shall be rewarded for your endeavors." Taking a deep breath, Elizabeth calmed herself. "Now, let us finish our meal."

The girls returned to eating. As their hunger was sated and the contents of the wine started to take effect, they began to slump in their chairs. Unable to resist the sleepiness that suddenly fell upon them, they slowly drifted onto the soft carpeted rug below them. Elizabeth watched the girls fall like feathers upon the ground as the sleeping juice began to serve its purpose. Humming to herself, she continued to eat until the last girl fell.

She finished her meal as she surveyed the girls slumped on the floor and then she finally called out to her servants, "Boian! Cat!" Two strong men obediently entered the dining hall. They were lean and muscular, having been hired by her husband to help with strenuous chores around the estate in his absence.

"Take these sleeping souls up to my chambers. Place them gently on my bed. If you find no more room, lay them on the couches. Ensure they are comfortable; I don't want to disturb their sleep."

Boian and Cat carried the slumbering waifs to their mistress' chambers as commanded. They dared not question the countess for fear of her husband's retribution upon his return. They looked at each other in silent rapport but did not utter a word as they finished their commission. They did not notice the translucent figure hovering by the hearth. Genie, too, was mystified by the sleeping girls.

Elizabeth rose from the table and sauntered to the staircase. With each sway of her hips, she formulated her diabolic plan. Unexplainable jealousy crept into her pores again as she went to her chambers. She tried to contain an unwavering urge to burst into the room.

*No*, she told herself, *what I am about to undertake must be done with great care.*

Quietly, she turned the handle on the door and pushed it away as she entered the room. She glanced at the Genie, and a smirk formed on her otherwise stoic face.

"What are your intentions, Elizabeth?" Genie had never questioned a master before. He was shocked that he did so now, but he needed to know what would happen to these young girls sprawled in various places around the room.

"What is it to you, Genie?" Elizabeth questioned indignantly. This Genie had been such a recluse, keeping to himself mainly, she didn't realize he had a conscience. "What I do with these girls is none of your concern. You told me the laws, and I am following them. Nothing I have asked of you goes against your rules. What I do with my own wishes is not for you to know. You may hang there, if you wish, to see what I will carry out, but you dare not interfere," she spat.

Genie's insides churned at her maliciousness. He felt ill again, just as he had before with the others.

*Why am I doomed to be tormented by the vileness of the human world?*

He could not fathom such loathing in the world. These truly were deadly sins of the flesh.

Since she had not requested her last wish, Genie was again trapped to witness the dastardly demonstration of her vileness. Once again, revolted by the urge to accompany Elizabeth in the actions she was about to carry out, dueling emotions tore at his core. He desperately wanted to fulfill her last wish and return to his prison, which seemed more like a sanctuary at times like this.

Elizabeth casually made her way to the chairs lined in a perfect circle around the fireplace. Gingerly, she picked up one of the embroidery needles and touched it to her forefinger. A tiny drop of blood appeared on her skin. She put the needle back in its place while sucking the blood away. Picking up a larger needle, she again pricked her finger. The wound it made was a fraction deeper than the first and caused her to wince. Though it was slightly painful, it still didn't produce the outcome she sought.

Frowning, she repeated the action with an even larger needle. This needle was used to sew massive tapestries, and therefore, it was much larger than its sisters. This time, Elizabeth pricked her wrist at the bend between her palm and lower arm. She pulled the needle back and jabbed it forward into her skin, careful not to pierce the blue line of the visible vein underneath. Blood gushed from the puncture. She cried out in pain and triumph, immediately bringing the damaged skin to her mouth. She drank the warm, red liquid, feeling it trickle down her throat, and smiled.

Pulling the injured wrist from her lips, she reached for the embroidery cloth and wrapped it around her wound to try and stop the bleeding. The wound was very deep, and soon the white canvas designed for beautiful artwork was soaked. She started to feel a little faint, so she sat in one of the chairs after pushing the materials away. While she sat, she contemplated her next move. She would need to work quickly before the sleeping juice she gave to the girls wore off.

*I should have used more in their wine*, she thought.

Elizabeth glanced at the curtained window in her room. She stood up, still feeling dizzy, and stumbled to the window. Throwing open the curtains, she saw the sun hanging low in the sky. *My last wish!* She needed to make her last wish before it dropped beneath the horizon. She whirled around, searching for Genie. She spotted him quietly observing her from a shadowed distance in the room.

"And now for my last request...wish as you called it," Elizabeth said, fixing her eyes upon his. Her words did not falter in the slightest. "I wish for a large, marble tub, placed also in my chambers, right over there," she pointed towards the middle of the circle, directly in front of the hearth. "Use whatever you call your magic, to keep the tub warm. I do not want to be cold when I sit inside it."

Genie, not wanting to be in Elizabeth's presence any longer than necessary, hastily granted her exact demand and flew back into his lamp with such force it toppled over, laying it on its side. Elizabeth ran to the lamp as the last of Genie vanished inside. She frantically tried to rub on it some more, enticing Genie to return. It was no use, once the wishes of the lamp's finder had been exhausted, the lamp would no longer produce anymore. Furious that she could not continue her demands, she tossed the lamp to the floor and turned to her dozing victims.

As she returned, her longing gazed over to the slumbering girls, and her rage at the Wishkeeper's sudden departure vanished from her thoughts like the snuff of a candle. Their smooth faces were still deep in sleep, unaware of the harm that was about to come to them. She inspected each girl, trying to decide whom to start with first. She lovingly caressed their faces as she examined them, feeling the softness and youth of their flawless skin. It was difficult to decide which one to begin with, but she finally settled on the smallest one first. The one resting peacefully in her bed; her husband's side of the bed. She started to picture the girl underneath her husband's naked body. Her demented mind's eye saw how he caressed her hair as he slowly thrust himself into her virgin pussy, causing a soft moan to escape her lips. He carefully increased his thrusts. His body glistened with sweat as he continued to pound the sweetness under him. Faster and faster, he drove himself into her until both let out a scream of ecstasy.

The imagined outburst brought Elizabeth out of her trance, and she raced towards the bed, roughly grabbing the girl by the wrist, and pulling her from the bed. Her body hit the floor with a resounding thud, but she did not wake. The drug still had its grasp on the poor girl. She dragged the unconscious waif into the circle and tried to hoist her into the tub. Even though Elizabeth had experienced some manual labor in the time her husband had been away, developing some strength, the girl's tiny frame proved to be difficult for Elizabeth to lift. Rage increased her zeal and with a loud grunt, she pushed the girl over the side of the tub.

Elizabeth debated on whether to remove the girl's dress; she would soon be weighed down from what she was about to do, and Elizabeth wasn't sure she had strength enough to lift her out of the tub when she had finished. She settled on removing her clothes. Her thoughts and body felt freer now that she wasn't encumbered by her attire. Standing there, unclothed, the vision of her husband and the tramp's lovemaking appeared in her thoughts. The two of them, writhing in lust, mocking her fueled her jealousy.

Rushing to the chairs, she grabbed the largest needle. The one that had done the most damage to her flesh. She returned to the girl and ripped the left sleeve off her dress with one pull, tearing the delicate material from its stitching. Elizabeth grabbed the limp, exposed arm, and searched for the large blue vein that ran from shoulder to wrist and plunged the needle in its center, carefully ensuring the girl's arm stayed within the confines of the tub. She quickly withdrew the needle and blood splurged from the punctured hole it had made.

Elizabeth fell back onto her backside, cackling as she watched the flow ooze into the tub. The flowing liquid found the girl's dress and quickly absorbed into the fabric.

"No!" Elizabeth screamed, regretting her decision not to remove the girl's clothes. She swiftly got up and pulled the girl from the tub. "Stupid girl," she hissed. "You were supposed to bleed in the tub, not on yourself." She stood up, grabbing the girl's hands, but she lost her grip from the slickness of the blood. Cursing under her breath, she tried again and, this time, managed to pull the girl out of the tub onto the floor, where she then dragged her body to the corner of the room. The girl did not stir as her life slowly poured out of her onto the floor. The docile image of her face would forever remain frozen in unconscious unawareness, blood wrapping itself around her like a warm, crimson blanket.

Regaining her composure, Elizabeth returned to the bed and yanked the clothes off her next victim. The adrenaline coursing through her gave her the strength of ten men. She would not make the mistake again of not disrobing the girl. As she hauled her towards the tub, but stopped suddenly when she heard a soft whimper coming from the chaise lounge, and she saw one of the girls stirring from her sleep. Panic struck as she whipped her head around the room listening for more sounds. She halted her progress, dropped the girl, and raced to the chairs, finding another large needle. She reached the wakening girl and stabbed her neck, one thrust after another until she heard no more sounds. Blood pooled beneath the girl's once-blonde curls, darkening the locks until they looked almost black.

Mesmerized, Elizabeth stood motionless, watching the blood flow quickly and then slowly as the muscles from the girl's heart could no longer pulse her life through her veins. "Serves you right," she spat at the pale face and returned to her task.

Elizabeth paused for a moment as she reached the tub.

*Maybe I should rethink this*, she pondered.

She needed a way to get the blood to fill the tub without exhausting herself by lifting the girls in and out of the tub. The idea finally came to her after much deliberation.

She lifted the girl into a sitting position, facing the tub. She then balanced the girl's left arm on the edge. Still holding the needle she had previously used; she once again plunged the sharp tip into the vein of the postulate girl. This time, she achieved the desired effect. Blood spilled into the tub.

Once all the life of each of the girls had spilled into the tub, Elizabeth gingerly stuck her toe into the deep, red liquid. True to his word, it had stayed warm. Not wanting to slip, she slowly eased her foot into the tub. When she finally finished entering the tub, she stood there, blood up to her knees, and looked down at the miniature lake of pure youth.

Her jealous rage subsided as she lowered herself into the warm surroundings. Her hand scooped the blood and she stared at it as it dripped over the edges of her palm. She used her other hand to cup another mass of the liquid, bringing her two hands together. Carefully, she lifted her hands to her face and let the crimson substance cascade over her cheeks. Never again would she feel inadequate or question her desirability. With the blood of virgins, she would forever maintain her youth. And there were plenty more virgins should she ever feel unwanted again.

After she finished bathing, Elizabeth got out of the tub and dressed herself, not caring that she was covered in blood. She walked over to the discarded lamp and picked it up. Cherry streaks stained the metal as she softly stroked its sides.

"Thank you, Genie," she softly whispered to the cold fixture.

She walked over to her dowry chest and wrapped it lovely back into the folds of the blue fabric from whence it came. Closing the lid of the chest, she then made her way to her bed. Laying down, Elizabeth closed her eyes and fell asleep.

# 15
# GENIE'S SUFFERING

**B**ack in his lamp, as Genie sat with his head in his hands, the weight of the witnessed horrors bore down on him like an unrelenting storm. His eyes, haunted by the scenes of pain and suffering, reflected the toll it had taken on him.

He had no idea what Elizabeth had wanted with the tub, nor did he care to know. The scene of those poor girls, sedated without a care in the world, not knowing their fate, gnawed at him, but he could not bring himself to think about it any longer. He pulled the memory from him and flicked it into the memory ball with such speed that he thought the sheer force would crack the delicate orb.

*That would be wonderful*, he thought.

He then had the terrorizing thought that the memories would find their way back to their owner – *him*, should the orb be destroyed.

The responsibilities thrust upon him were far beyond the whimsical granting of wishes; they were demands that shook the very core of his being. He grappled with the conflict between his compassionate nature and the compulsion to carry out actions that went against everything he stood for. Or did it? He still harbored vile desires as he watched Elizabeth prick her skin with the needle. He further felt a twinge of euphoria as he saw her draw the blood out with her lips.

"Stop!" he bellowed at the conflict in his mind, shaking the furniture so hard it moved from its position on the floor.

Despite the twisted longings in his heart, Genie knew that he had to find a way to navigate through the darkness that surrounded him. The choices before him were like a labyrinth of moral ambiguity, and the consequences of each step resonated in the air like an ominous echo.

Genie vowed to himself that he would no longer succumb to these abhorrent thoughts. The next master to unleash him would not manipulate him into some despicable terror scheme. He would find a way to persuade the new master not to wreak havoc on the innocent. He would defy the dark forces that sought to exploit his powers and reclaim agency over his own existence. He wondered if there was a loophole in the rules of these ungodly powers he possessed that he could exploit to defy any malicious wish a master spoke.

His anger over his turmoil seemed to have soothed him. It was as if a switch had been turned on inside his subconscious. He found himself able to cope with the two conflicting emotions raging a war for his approval. He could live with both. He had the power to decide which he gave into; which one would rule his thoughts. The simplicity that good and evil could coexist in him without him losing himself to evil alleviated so much angst. He just needed to see more good in the world. More kindness. More altruism.

Time stood still for Genie as he pondered away at the notion until the lamp stirred again, signaling his release into the world. His idea of testing the protocols would soon be revealed to him. Unfortunately, his next master lacked any qualities Genie had hoped to see more of. In fact, his next master would be the most diabolical one he had ever seen.

# 16

# JACK

Jack had been walking along the East End District of London after class. Darkness shrouded the main streets and alleyways, a time when sordid people made their way into discarded society. Sloppy drunkards with their disheveled shirts and disease-ridden prostitutes littered doorways along the avenue. Occasionally, rats the size of domestic cats could be seen scurrying to and from in the search for whatever crumbs they could find.

It was late August, and a recent rain produced a wet sheen along the cobblestones. The stones' heat and the rain's coolness had caused steam to rise, making an eerie scene between the shadow and the dotted street lamps along the road. Anyone wandering the streets was sure to feel the moisture of sweat as it trickled down their faces and covered the recesses of their skin.

The sticky, wet air had crept into the classroom, where he had just left his studies of medicine and human anatomy. It had absorbed all the smells of decaying cadavers, embalming fluids, and sweat, leaving Jack smelling like a walking dead man. He badly needed a bath to rid himself of the stench.

Although the summer months always left him with lingering, pungent odors, he enjoyed his studies. There was something about dead, rotten flesh that intrigued him. The way it now peeled and stretched away from the body where it once covered its owner in a perfect symbiotic state. When his professor or fellow students weren't watching him, he would softly caress the lifeless skin. He wondered what it would be like to be able to cut into a live body and not one that didn't bleed any longer. He fantasized about cutting into living flesh, slicing the body from the sternum to the crotch. He even imagined the newly invented anesthesia wearing off and the patient waking up while they were being cut open. The thought made Jack's cock harden. He was thankful his lab coat covered his twisted desires.

Jack hurried along the alley, increasing his pace each time one of the degenerates would step forward either begging for coins or soliciting their bodies for profit. He wanted to get home and relieve himself from his most recent encounter with a freshly delivered corpse. It was that of a young woman who had died from syphilis. The thought of her fucking so many men that she had contracted the deadly disease made Jack sick but horny at the same time. He imagined himself as one of her lovers. His professor had slapped him in front of his classmates when he saw Jack playing with his cock through the pocket of his trousers.

As he continued his walk, one disgraceful creature timidly approached him, breaking him from his erotic thoughts. With one long, vertical glance, he could tell that she hadn't been on the streets for very long. Her garments were mostly clean and intact, not the usual tattered dress of a lady of the night. Her hair was long, dark, and still neatly combed. And, she didn't smell like the others he had encountered before.

"Hey there, handsome," her voice faltered between confidence and modesty. "Want some of this?" Grabbing the edge of her bodice, she tugged it down, revealing her soft, white breast, but not enough to expose all of her bosom or nipple. The gesture confirmed Jack's suspicions that this lady of the night was merely a novice in the art of sexual prowess.

Normally, on nights like these, Jack walked away from unsolicited invitations. Something about this one made him stop. He motioned for the girl to come closer. He thought of the girl lying on the cold slab in the laboratory. Their similarities intrigued him.

"What are you offering this evening?" He reached out his hand, grabbed her breast, and squeezed.

The girl winced from the pressure of his grip but did not cry out or turn away. She needed the money tonight and business had recently slowed. She didn't like this line of work, but she had been given no choice. Her employer at the textile mill had recently cut everyone's wages. Poverty ran rampant throughout the city and she, like so many others, wasn't immune to it. Too many people and not enough jobs drove the economy into despair and the foremen of the all-too-few workhouses took advantage of it. People were willing to work for any amount they could, so why should the business owners cut into their profits by paying higher wages? If workers didn't like their salary, they would be let go without much explanation, let alone the earned wages of the day. The owners sat in their plush houses, eating the finest foods while their workers starved. The girl before him was no exception. The only thing she could do to supplement her income and feed her family was to sell the parts of her that men like Jack wanted under the blind eye of proper society.

Pulling Jack's harsh grip from her breast, she guided his hand lower until it reached the triangular fold of her flimsy gown. Pushing his hand up to her crotch, she began to grind on his fingers, moaning softly. She had been told that moaning gave men a sense of accomplishment in fulfilling a woman's desire, making the customer feel more masculine.

"Whatever you want, sugar," she whispered in his ear. Her tongue softly licked his sensitive skin, and Jack involuntarily shuttered at the sensation.

"That's exactly what you're going to find out." Jack pulled the girl with him down the darkened street to an alleyway off the beaten path. He quickly found a small shop that had closed for the evening. He shoved the prostitute inside. He didn't want to be seen even though no one would give their departure a second glance.

"What's your name?" he asked when they were far enough away from the sketchy nightlife of the ill-reputed community. He had found a boutique that had closed for the night. The contents of women's hats, scarves, and fine linen adorned the tiny, darkened space. Jack caressed the soft fabrics, vaguely listening to the girl.

"Mary Jane," she said, "but people call me Polly." She tried her best to be coquettish, a trait she had difficulty pulling off.

A stiff drink would help, she thought to herself. She wondered if her newly found customer had any whiskey with him. He looked to be the type of man who would hide a flask of the comforting beverage. She hesitated but asked anyway.

"You got any liquor?" Her eager eyes pleaded for something to calm her nerves.

"No," he said irritated by her question. "And if I did, I wouldn't give you any. I want you to feel with every fiber of your being what I plan to do with you."

A touch of fear crept into Polly's eyes. She had had rough men before and had been able to handle herself with them. Mainly, they had been too drunk to cause any harm or injury. Most of them couldn't even complete the job. Since her husband had separated from her, she could only meet her lustful cravings through the deplorable men that blindly groped her satisfying only themselves in their inebriated fucks. She would finish herself with her own hands as she watched their impotent cocks hanging between their legs long after they had passed out. Being a prostitute enabled her to feed her family and get off. It had taken a while to get to this point, past the vulgarity of selling herself. She still didn't like it but had to admit it sometimes had its perks.

The man before her was not drunk, however. In fact, he was very virile. Part of her was excited at her alarm. Her good-for-nothing husband surely didn't exhibit such awe. This man had an air of arrogance. The way he confidently directed her caused a sudden splurge of wetness between her thighs. She squirmed with anticipation as she felt the warm liquid trickle down her leg.

Jack immediately caught pleasure in her eyes; the way she parted her lips in readiness started to have a negative effect on him. He slapped her hard across her face, instantly wiping away her lascivious thoughts. She gasped in horror.

"What was that for?" she asked, cradling her stinging cheek.

"Because you are not going to enjoy this. I am." Jack punched her ribs this time. She toppled over in pain.

"Please. Please don't," she whimpered.

"Don't worry," he told her. "I'll pay you well for your services. You won't have to worry about eating for the next month."

Polly wasn't sure she could endure any more blows, no matter how much money he promised. She already had started to feel the soreness in her lips and ribs.

"Get on the floor and spread your legs, bitch," he snarled.

Polly did as he commanded. As she positioned herself, shaking with fear as she lay on the floor, she watched him frantically scan the room as if something had caught his attention. She absently wondered what he was searching for. Abruptly, stepping away from her, her gaze followed him as he crossed the small space. He reached for an odd object he had spotted. Something she had never seen before.

Jack picked up the peculiar piece and inspected its making. It was hard to make out in the darkness. He felt around different countertops in search of candles or any light. Finding nothing of use, he brought it close to the petite storefront window hoping to get a better look.

Polly could barely see what Jack was holding. It looked to be some lamp. She wondered if it had oil in it for lighting. It was so dark in the tiny shop, not that she wanted to endure this man's advances in any light. For now, his concentration was on the lamp and not her. She contemplated escaping. She could easily slip out the door while his concentration was elsewhere, but the thought of money kept her in her place.

Polly watches as Jack rubbed the lower part of his palm against the shiny metal. It began to warm and vibrate. As the vibrations became stronger, he almost dropped it. Instead, he quickly placed it on a nearby table. A cloudy mist emerged from the lamp until it formed before him. Polly gasped as she watched it fill the room.

"I am the genie of the lamp," Genie bellowed, taking in his surroundings once again. He immediately spotted a young woman lying bare-legged on the floor. He then looked at the man standing before him—the one who summoned him from the lamp—the one he must now call Master. He finished reciting his well-rehearsed speech once again.

*No need to touch this one's forehead*, Genie sadly surmised.

He could smell the evil that oozed from this one's pores. He began his mandated speech.

# 17

# JACK'S WRATH

J ack silently listened to what this self-named Genie presented
to him. It took a moment for Genie's words to register any
comprehension. He closed his eyes, digesting the words. Had he
understood this apparition correctly? His mind began tumbling
ideas around. He glanced back at Polly. He had been in the throes
of forcing himself on this woman. He was ready to inflict pain
and punishment as he satisfied his desire. The appearance of this
ghastly being squelched that. *For now.*

Seeing Polly with her mouth agape in astonishment at the
sudden appearance of this creature turned Jack's thoughts back to
the act he was about to perform. He felt himself harden, imagining
his cock inside her warm, wet hole. His mind raced between finding out more about this genie and releasing the passion stirring
inside him. He decided to focus on the latter.

"You can't stop me from doing what I want, correct?" He
pointed his finger at Genie.

"No. I can't stop you from doing what you want."

Genie desperately wanted to touch Jack's forehead to find out
exactly what he referred to, but he had been bamboozled before
when he had touched Vlad. He didn't want to know this man's
future, or anything he was determined to do. His lofty notion of
trying to dissuade his masters from causing harm flew from his

thoughts. He accepted he was powerless to do anything but stand by and be a spectator of this forced demonic slavery.

"Good." With confirmation, Jack turned on his heels and returned to Polly but not before picking up a pair of scissors from the table packed with unsewn bolts of colorful fabrics. Reaching Polly, he swiftly cut off her dress exposing the rest of her undergarments to his lustful eyes.

He stood back up and unbuttoned his breeches, pulling them off, one leg at a time. Still clothed in his undergarment, he used the scissors to cut them, freeing his hard cock. A trickle of blood ran down one leg as he cut himself in his haste. He didn't care. The sight of blood intensified his desire.

Jack grabbed Polly's undergarment and slashed it open. He then grabbed her by her hips and flipped her onto her knees. Dropping himself to her level, he clasped his hands on either side of her lush hips. With one angry push, he brutally forced his cock inside her anus. Polly screamed in agony. A sound so piercingly painful it made Genie wince when he heard it.

Jack paid no mind to Polly's protests as he continued to slam into her. He found excitement in her pain. Having Genie watching added to his glorification. Grunting, he gave one final thrust, climaxing. The release sent him spinning in euphoria.

Jack violently pulled out of her and pushed her weepy body further to the floor with such force that she smashed her face into the hard surface. She heard the pop of a tooth as it cracked from the impact. Blood began to leak from her mouth. The previous excitement she felt before having rough sex quickly left her. She felt violated and embarrassed that she had expected something far different than what had just occurred.

As Jack was temporarily distracted by his own satisfaction, Genie tried to gain Polly's attention. It was no use. Her long, dark locks of hair hid her face as her bent-over body racked with pain from the abuse could only remain still even though the assault was over.

Focusing back on reality, Jack rose from his slouched position, unashamed by his nudeness. He had never felt so alive before. Never in his wildest dreams did he expect such intoxicating ecstasy. The sex, the blood, the instilled fear. All of it combined to give him the greatest orgasm he had ever had. And now with the Genie's help, he could continue this pleasure trip.

Catching his breath, Jack contemplated what to do next and what his first wish would be. Not wanting to stop his summit of bliss, he wondered how he could continue it. He focused on what had given him the greatest pleasure. Was it fucking or causing pain? Genie couldn't help with the fucking. He was quite capable of performing through his own will, as he had just demonstrated. This genie couldn't help with the infliction of pain either, as he had purposely stated before.

*What could a genie do?* He pondered.

He had a thought. *What if I could cause more pain? Would that intensify my pleasure?*

He returned to Polly, straddling her on his knees, and decided to test his theory. Without warning, he drove the point of the scissors between the blades of Polly's shoulders. Polly let out a bloodcurdling scream. The piercing cry of anguish hardened Jack's cock once again. As she writhed in pain, he let out a cry of delight mocking her.

Genie tried to move forward to help the poor soul but was held in his place by the forces of his own prison. He could only helplessly observe the heinous crime unfolding before him.

Jack slid himself behind Polly, hoisting her hips with one arm drawing her to him. He still held the scissors in his opposite hand. He pushed her resistant pussy onto his hardness as she continued to moan in pain. With each thrust of his cock, he ravaged her tender skin with the scissors until she lay motionless and muted, but still alive. Barely.

Covered in her splattering blood, Jack continued his slaughter until he finally released himself for a second time. He pulled out of her and sat back on his haunches, breathless and sated, his white seed mixing with the blood in a pinkish swirl at the base of her crotch.

"I must have this again," he gasped, desperately trying to slow his breathing. As he sat there, he concluded that his experiment of importance revealed that the greatest pleasure would be derived from both pain and fucking at the same time. He turned to Genie.

"I'm ready to give you my first wish."

"I wish for the finest knife a blacksmith can make." There was no emotion in his request. He asked for the knife as one would ask for an extra helping of potatoes. The knife instantly appeared in his hand. He examined the metal and the handle, both crafted in an excellent combination of steel and leather.

"Master," Genie interrupted Jack's admiration of the blade. "Why would you desire such an instrument? Wouldn't you rather have money or...or food...or jewelry?" Genie tried his best to turn the unmistakably deviant thoughts in Jack's mind into something less sinister.

Jack gently ran his thumb over the edge of the blade. A small droplet of blood appeared where the sharp edge had been cut.

"Now, why would I want any of those things you mentioned? I have exactly what I want right here in my hand." His eyes darted to Genie. Slightly bowing his head, yet maintaining his piercing gaze, his mouth formed a devilish grin.

Breaking away from the enthralled trance of his magical weapon, Jack strode over to the broken figure on the floor. His foot kicked a strategic blow to Polly's ribs. She screamed out in pain with the remaining life she had in her. The sound aroused him immediately. He fought to control his need to take her again. Instead, he pulled her head up by her long, brown hair, exposing her neck.

With one smooth slice, he cut her throat. The acute sharpness of the blade made it feel like slicing through butter. Polly couldn't scream. The only sound was that of gurgling as the blood sprayed across the floor in time with her rapidly diminishing heartbeat. He casually dressed himself as he watched the blood ebb away from its lifeless owner.

Although Genie had turned away before Jack committed the heinous crime, he couldn't escape the noise of Polly slowly dying as her life emptied onto the beautiful rug beneath her head. Under his breath, he repeatedly cursed Divine-Genie for his predicament. He had tried to dissuade Jack, but that proved futile. Two more wishes awaited his command. He didn't know how much more of this he could take. He wondered what would happen if he took the knife from Jack and put an end to his own misery. He extended his smoky hand towards the knife in an attempt to snatch it from Jack before he could inflict any more damage to the lifeless body under him. Jack noticed the move immediately.

"Oh, you want this?" he sneered. "Come get it!" Tauntingly, he waved the knife before Genie, daring him to take it.

It was a futile effort. Genie could no more grab the knife than he could convince Jack, or anyone else for that matter, not to commit horrible acts upon their fellow man. The knife passed through Genie's hand like the wind through an open window.

Jack's demented cackle echoed in Genie's ear. "Nice try, ghost."

Rejecting Genie's disdain, Jack turned back to Polly. His academic pursuance drove his sights to her abdomen. He could examine her without the scorn of his teachers always looking over him as they had in the classroom. Turning her over onto her back, he used the knife to cut away the remainder of her bloodied dress. His desire to fuck her again returned, but he quickly pushed it away, concentrating on the next step in his mutilation. Carefully, he used the knife to carve into her flesh, making the precision cuts as he had learned. He peeled back the layers of skin, exposing her organs. He reached down and picked up her stomach. Cradling the warm gob, he inspected the organ. Somehow, it was bigger than the stomach of the long-dead specimens he studied. This anomaly piqued his curiosity. He wanted to inspect the other organs to see if they also were larger but was interrupted by sounds coming from the alleyway.

Jack hurried to his feet, slipping on the slick, sticky pools of blood. He couldn't be discovered here, covered in blood with a butchered woman. He reached the door and opened it, quickly sneaking out but not before throwing money on the floor next to Polly, keeping his promise to pay her. Darkness concealed his escape, and he trotted down the road away from the sounds of a gathering crowd. He turned the corner just as he heard voices shouting for the police. He paused between two buildings listening for any movement towards him. Hearing none, he casually stepped into the dark street that concealed his bloodstained clothes. He smirked at the frantic commotion of the discovery of his work. His interrupted work, he corrected himself.

Still feeling exhilarated by his ghastly accomplishments, Jack almost skipped toward his home. He reached into his pocket and withdrew some coins for the beggar outside his gate. His blood-crusted fingers handed the poor creature enough for some ale and maybe a slice of day-old bread for the night. Crossing the threshold of his flat, he closed the door as Genie floated in behind him.

"That was splendid!" he told Genie. He rambled on about his grotesque feat as if Genie hadn't even been there to be witness to it. Genie patiently waited for Jack to finish his tale.

"Do you have your second wish in mind yet, Master?" he inquired. He needed this ordeal to be over as quickly as possible.

"I most certainly do, my dear chap." He reached out as if to slap Genie on the back jovially before realizing it was useless. Shrugging off the mistake, he presented Genie with his next wish.

"For my second wish, I require an entire set of knives like the one I used on Polly. I'm exhausted from trying to cut the flesh of my anatomy subjects with the dull, rusted instruments they expect students to use. They are worthless pieces of metal. I want to be the envy of my schoolmates. I want these knives to be of different lengths and have varying blade angles. I want them all to fit in slotted compartments of a leather case that I can fold and carry unnoticed."

"Your wish has been granted," was all Genie said.

Instantly, the satchel of knives appeared on the table next to Jack. The soft leather was open to reveal the various blades, as Jack had requested. He picked each knife up and inspected the craftsmanship of the instrument. The assortment of knife blades was exceptionally straight to curved like a crescent moon. When he had finished scrutinizing every single blade, his hands were once again covered in fresh blood from the cuts he had made, testing their sharpness.

"Very good, Genie. Yes, very good," he lovingly said.

Genie had no doubts about what Jack intended to do with the knives. He longed for a way to stop this madness that had befallen Jack. Maybe it was the wishes causing the madness, he pondered. If that were so, though, he would be the reason for all the turmoil in his masters. He became sick with guilt. There would have been no victims if he hadn't granted their wishes. No one would have had to suffer so much from his cursed gift.

"And for my last wish," Jack's voice broke Genie from the silent tormented war he waged inside his head. He had been thinking of that poor girl Jack had so brutally violated and then murdered. He thought about what her children would do now that their mother had been taken from them. Oh, yes, he knew about Polly. Somehow, he knew.

"For my last wish," Jack started again, this time looking Genie directly in the eyes. "Next Saturday, I wish to dine at Simpson's in the Strand at 5 o'clock in the evening. I want a reservation for one. I want enough money to cover the price of my meal and a drink—make that two drinks. I also want a finely tailored, dark suit to wear for the occasion, with gold cufflinks and a proper gold watch."

"Such an unusual request." Genie hadn't realized he had spoken the thought aloud.

Jack sneered, "You don't think me worthy to dine at such an establishment? Or to wear such fine clothing?"

"Master, I meant to convey that I found the request unexpected." He prayed Jack would leave it at that and not question him further. What he had truly meant was that he had expected Jack to ask for something much more diabolical, given what he had wanted for his first two wishes. Jack, thankfully, did not press the subject further. Genie began his descent back into the lamp.

"Wait!" Jack yelled as he watched Genie start to disappear. "What about my last wish? Don't you want to see it carried out?"

"No. I do not. Your wish has been granted. Next Saturday, at 5 o'clock in the evening, go to Simpson's in the Strand. The maître-d will be waiting for your arrival." With that, he vanished from sight. The lamp shuttered and sat quietly on the table next to the satchel of knives.

Jack scooped up the lamp. "You had better not betray me, Genie," he hissed at the container.

Annie finished cleaning Lady Kent's apartment and was getting ready to leave when she noticed the brandy bottle sitting by the cabinet. She peered around the corner of the room into the hallway, looking for the home's occupants. She was met with silence. The only audible sound was Lady Kent softly snoring in the chaise lounge in the study down the hall.

Tiptoeing into the dining room, she grabbed the bottle and tilted its opening towards her lips. The brandy felt smooth as the liquid glided down her throat. It had been hours since her last drink, and her hands had started to shake from the withdrawal effects. She usually didn't have to wait so long between drinks, but Lady Kent had been unusually picky about how Annie had been attending to her chores lately. She had suspected Annie of drunkenness, but never could quite catch her in the act.

Annie had many years of practice at hiding her love of alcohol. Her father had given her the first taste of alcohol at age seven. Her soldier father thought it amusing to watch his young daughter stumble around the place in a drunken stupor. Her siblings were not so entertained. Over the years, they had tried to persuade Annie to give up drinking. Try as she may, she always returned to warm, welcoming, liquid happiness.

After three hefty servings of the brandy, Annie replaced the bottle from where she found it and exited the room. Ever so softly, she opened the house's front door and staggered slightly down the marble steps. Regaining her footing, she made her way down the street.

She passed several establishments and was tempted to stop in to top off the brandy with an ale or two, but kept walking, fighting the urge. She passed one window where she could see patrons enjoying an evening meal. Her stomach grumbled. Her alcohol consumption suppressed her appetite, but the smells of the food wafting through the open door of the restaurant caused her stomach to grumble with hunger.

Her eyes fixed on a man sitting alone at one of the tables. He was a handsome man; finely dressed in a dark suit with gold cufflinks. She wondered why he hadn't had any company with him. As if drawn to the man, she entered the restaurant. The host stopped her before she could go on.

"Do you have reservations, Miss?" he inquired. He could smell the alcohol and didn't want any trouble from the likes of this one.

"Oh, I do apologize. That is my husband over there," she pointed at the single patron. "I was late getting here from my employment this evening and didn't accompany him when he came in." She smiled at the host, batting her eyelashes in a feigned flirting attempt to persuade him to let her pass.

Skeptically, the host stared at her momentarily before letting her through. Annie sauntered over to the table. The man looked up from his meal, puzzled by the bodacious woman before him staring at him, smiling.

"Hi. I'm Annie," she said coyly. "I saw you from outside and wondered why such a handsome man like yourself would want to dine alone. I just had to come inside and convince you to let me join you. What's your name, sweetie?"

"Jack," he said politely.

"Do you mind if I sit down, Jack, and join you for dinner?" Her eyes sparkled with anticipation.

His voice dropped to a low octave and with a slow, determined, almost lustful tone, he answered her, "No, Annie, I don't mind at all."

# 18
# GENIE'S HUMILITY

Genie felt numb, not from the chill, but from witnessing Jack's actions. His mind and body were devoid of sensation, drained by the sight of Jack's deeds, leaving him hollow of all emotions. It was as though the universe itself had become a cosmic pugilist, delivering blows from every angle until he lay as an unconscious opponent, battered and beaten. Even draining the memories of Polly into the orb wouldn't erase all that he felt. Jack had been worse than all his previous masters. He had seemed to enjoy what he was doing maliciously. The others seemed to be merely experimenting with their cruelty; Jack relished its existence. He demonically matured with each kill. He was the devil in human form.

He wandered aimlessly around the prisoned lamp. He ate, even though he needed no sustenance. He even tried to drown his woeful mind in liquor. It had no effect. Nothing saved him from his melancholy. Moving through time into the modern world, he acquired some entertainment such as puzzles and board games. They gave some small measure of enjoyment, especially the board games. They reminded him of his youth and his mortal life. He wished he could return to that life and make different choices. He couldn't even say whether he would have wished for anything or simply thrown the lamp far from him when Divine-Genie first emerged.

Time moved on, but for Genie, nothing changed. Day in and day out, he followed the same routine. Occasionally, he would peer into the memory orb, recalling every wish granted. He pondered the naivety of persuading the masters to wish for something else. It didn't matter, those wretched beings could no more turn from their fate than he could. He reconciled with himself that it didn't matter what he would have tried, their minds were made up long before he appeared to them. He succumbed to the fact that no good people were left in the world.

He dreamed of his life after his wishes were finished. A thought he tried to avoid. It seemed he would be doomed to this fate for eternity. Maybe eternity was what it would take for mortals to realize their stupidity of hate and violence. It would take forever for them to understand their common bonds and learn to live in harmony with one another.

He missed the sound of laughter most of all. In his mortal life, he would laugh with his friends. He could be silly, and no one would think less of him. He could play pranks on his brothers and sisters, and they would join in on the fun. He missed his family. They died ages ago. He wondered if they thought of him and why he had disappeared. He wondered if they missed him, too.

A tear fell from Genie's eye. He was sad about his life and his choices. Before his emotions gave way to sobbing, he felt the familiar rattle of the lamp. He didn't want to do this again, and he didn't want to witness any more horror. What he wanted didn't matter; his curse continued, and he floated out of the lamp.

# 19

# ELEANOR

It was Anna's, or Eleanor as she preferred to be addressed, last day at finishing school. She missed New York and longed to be home, but she knew she'd miss the Academy even more. London had become her second home after her tragedy. She had also become close friends with the headmistress, Marie. Marie was full of life and aptitude. And she didn't give a shit about the power men wanted to exude over the, in their minds, weaker sex. A trait scorned by early 20th-century society. After all, women should know their place.

Eleanor admired Marie's courage to stand up to these pompous asses who felt all women were good for was to have babies and tend to the household while they indulged in drinks, cigars, and occasional bedroom frolicking with women who did not share their last name. Marie would call out these men, sometimes in a not-so-private setting. Eleanor would watch from afar. Afterward, she and Marie would laugh at the contemptuous looks she had received from other women but mostly from the men. The wives, on the other hand, had a much more enraged look, especially if it were their husbands who had been publicly chastised.

"I don't want to leave, Marie," Eleanor cried into her pillow.

"I know, darling, but you must. Your grandmother wants to show you off to society. Just think of the ball you will have. I hear it will be at the Waldorf-Astoria." Marie put her hand to her chest and fluttered her eyelashes.

"Oh, you know I care not of those things," Eleanor shrugged. "My family may have money but good looks and what society thinks of me matter not."

"Darling, you are a beautiful person. Why do you constantly think otherwise?"

"I'd prefer not to talk about it."

Eleanor's mother was never affectionate with her when she was a child. She knew her mother thought her looks were too plain for someone born into wealth and status. It was an attribute she harbored in herself later in life when she became a mother.

*Mother.* The thought of her mother made her sad. Even though her mother hadn't shown her the affection and love a child craved, her death had a profound effect on Eleanor. She had only been six when her mother died, and not six months later, her brother died of the same disease that took their mother. Her father, an alcoholic, had been sent away.

"Granny loves me though," she volunteered. "She stepped in when Mama and Papa abandoned me." Her voice lowered to a whisper as she spoke of her parents. The emotional scar caused by their actions was apparent.

"Of course, she does!" Marie exclaimed. "Why don't you come with me to my room? I have a going away present for you that I think will bring some cheer into your gloomy demeanor."

The two women made their way to Marie's room. They had spent countless nights here discussing the latest politics, religion, and women's rights, or lack thereof—conversations deemed not proper topics in public settings. Eleanor had always become passionate about the adversity regarding women not being allowed to vote. It was as if they were not considered intellectual enough to choose who they thought should run the country they were citizens of.

Marie reached the chest at the foot of her large four-poster, mahogany bed. As headmistress, she had the finest room at the Academy, even though Eleanor had much more money, she slept in the same quarters as the other girls. It was always a treat to visit Marie's room.

"Look at this," she said as she presented Eleanor with a lavish-looking lamp. "Isn't it just exquisite?"

Eleanor took the lamp from Marie and inspected its finery. She had never seen something so beautiful. It looked ancient, yet the gems shined like they had just been attached to the piece.

"It's lovely," she said. "What is it?"

"It's some sort of oil lamp, I think," Marie answered. "I picked it up in the market the other day when the weather was nice. The man said it originally came from Persia and was said to have magical powers. I'm certain he was joking and probably just wanted to make a sale."

"Hmm," Eleanor scoffed. "I'm sure you're right. What are these inscriptions on the sides between the gems?" She started to use the cuff of her sleeve to rub the lamp and inspect the odd drawings more closely.

"Don't rub it!" Marie warned. Laughing at her shock, Marie calmly spoke. "The man said you shouldn't rub it if you don't want the magic to come out."

"Marie," Eleanor laughed. "I've never known you to be superstitious."

"Well, I'm not. But there was something in the man's words that made me a little cautious."

"Then why on Earth did you buy it?"

"Because I thought that you would appreciate it. Something beautiful to remind you that you are beautiful," she countered.

"It is beautiful, and I thank you, my friend. I shall think of you whenever I look at it."

The two of them finished the day milling over Eleanor's ball, which she would be presented to society. They talked about the eligible bachelors who would inevitably vie for a dance or two with her, mostly because they wanted to be part of the socialite life that would come should they marry into her family. Their laughter could be heard throughout the halls of the Academy well into the night.

## Ten Years Later

Eleanor hadn't considered her life at the Academy in a long time. She was met with a whirlwind life when she returned to New York. Now, a wife and a mother, she felt a calling for something more. Like her mother, she didn't consider herself a very good caretaker of her child. She thought about Marie and the times when they would talk about how they would change the world if given the opportunity. And now, with her husband a very powerful man, she could use that status to do just that.

Sifting through boxes in her closet, she came upon the lamp Marie had given her. It still held its luxurious sheen. She recalled Marie's warning. Laughing at the silliness of her irrational belief in magic, Eleanor rubbed the lamp. At first, she thought she was imagining the tingling she felt in her hands until it became strong enough, she couldn't ignore it. A puff of smoke started to pour from the shaft's opening. The misty cloud grew larger until it formed the shape of a man. A man the likes of Eleanor could never have envisioned. She nearly collapsed when he spoke.

"I am the genie of the lamp..."

Mouth agape, Eleanor could not speak. Her mind raced with words, but they would not exit the dryness of her mouth. Marie was right! It was magical! Rubbing her eyes as if it was all a dream, Eleanor looked again. The misty being was still there.

Closing her mouth, she tried to conjure up enough spit to moisten the inside of her mouth enough to speak. When she felt she had readied herself, she addressed Genie.

"If I heard you correctly, you're a wish maker. Am I right?" she timidly but assuredly, asked.

"Yes," Genie said. Thinking of Elizabeth, his stomach churned at the sight of another woman. Could she be anywhere near as horrible as Elizabeth had been?

"I can have three wishes, you say? And, if I choose, I can use my last wish to free you. Is that correct?"

Genie stared at this woman, puzzled at the mention of his potential freedom. No one had mentioned the idea of freeing him before, and even he had given up hope of ever leaving his cursed enslavement.

"Why is it no one has freed you? How long have you been this way?" Eleanor inquired with sincere interest. After her initial shock, she wanted to know more about this genie, as he called himself. Thanks to Marie, she had always been a direct person, never one to back down from a dispute. She was intrigued by this conundrum before her. Having had her views and opinions rejected simply because of her sex, she felt a camaraderie with Genie.

"I have been cursed with this reluctant gift for over two thousand years," Genie mournfully replied. "It was my own greed as a young boy that put me in this predicament. You do not want to know what I have been forced to endure and forced to grant."

"Go on," she softly pleaded.

Genie lowered himself from above to the carpet where Eleanor sat. She crossed her legs to get comfortable as if she were a child ready to hear an enticing story. Genie had her full attention. Genie mirrored her posture, floating a fraction above the floor.

"I apologize for my nervousness. No one has ever asked me how I felt about all this."

"Well, now someone has. Tell me anything you are comfortable sharing," Eleanor gently pushed.

"Hmm, where to begin?" Genie toyed with his misty beard. He could make solid contact with himself but not with anything in the mortal world. Eleanor was fascinated by the movement.

"I was a young boy when I came into this situation," he began. "Young and naïve, to be honest. I thought I wanted what my father had. He was a wealthy man, and I mistook his wealth for greed. I was greedy and didn't want to put in the work my father had all his life to attain what I saw as fortune. He attained what he had the hard way. I wanted to take the easy way out. That was my biggest mistake."

Genie and Eleanor sat in silence for a moment before Genie spoke again. He was surprised by her patience and attentiveness. Her aura reflected a genuine interest and compassion. He mused something he hadn't felt since...well since he existed. He wanted to continue but was afraid he would scare her if he told her all he had witnessed. He decided to gloss over the horror and skim the surface of what his life had truly been like since he adopted this new form.

"Eleanor," he began again, "I don't want to trouble you with all I have seen. Let us just leave it as is. I haven't had the best of times for the past two thousand years. The masters I have had were terrible people, the likes I am sure you have never had in your company. But, my guilt, my displeasure of this whole curse, has been that I feel responsible for their crimes. I granted their wishes. I made them do those horrible, obscene things to innocent people. I feel their crime is just as much as mine is."

Eleanor thought for a moment, taking in all that Genie had said, his composure, and his internal turmoil.

"Genie," she whispered softly but sternly, "it has been my experience that people are who they are. They are given certain circumstances in which they have to make a decision. Good or bad, the decision is theirs and theirs alone. You can choose to do good in this life you're given, or you can choose to do bad. You did not create the Masters you had to become monsters. They were already monsters who took advantage of a precious opportunity to elicit the situation to fit their demented minds. You are not at fault for this."

"I wish I could share your conclusions."

"I will show you what they should have done." She abruptly stood up, threw her shoulders back, and tilted her head sternly up, facing Genie. "I am ready to make my first wish."

# 20

# ELEANOR'S HUMANITY

G enie braced himself. His experience had jaded him against expecting benevolence in people. Surely, Eleanor was not going to be any different than the others. She had just been stringing him along. She was going to wish for something heinous, want to inflict harm. He just knew it. He felt it in his porous bones.

"I know you said that my wishes must be granted before sunset. Does this mean that what I wish for must happen before sunset, or can I wish for something now that wouldn't take place until after sunset, like years from now?" she asked.

Genie had never been presented with such an odd request. He had always complied with what the masters had wanted then and there. He was noticeably puzzled at the quandary. He also didn't know the answer.

*What would happen if I agreed to grant her wish that wouldn't take place until further the future than a single day, and it wasn't allowed?* He wondered. *Would some cosmic explosion occur because I didn't fulfill the wish?*

Eleanor watched as Genie mentally debated her question. She thought it was a straightforward question. It puzzled her too, as to why no one else had thought of it. It must be a hard thing to request three wishes in such a short time frame. Maybe the forces that created this magic wanted them to be performed immediately hence the sunrise to sunset window of time. Maybe it was to make certain that one's wishes were a spur-of-the-moment type thing and not allow the grantee to think too long and hard over it. Whatever the reason, Genie seemed stumped at the question.

"To be honest, Eleanor, I have no answer to your question," Genie finally spoke. He thought back to Jack and his wish for dinner arrangements. He shuddered involuntarily at the thought. He had no idea whether or not Jack's dinner wish had come to fruition. He assumed it had as he was in Eleanor's presence rather than still at Jack's command. "I will grant your future wish with the understanding that it may not come to fruition. If you agree to these terms, ask away."

"That seems to be a fair answer," she replied. "With the assumption that my wish will eventually come to be, I wish to be involved in a humanitarian effort to help those less fortunate. I want to be involved in helping women become equal in society. I want to assist the impoverished. I want to put an end to child labor. No child should have to help supplement their family's income and they surely should not have to work in deplorable conditions simply because they are thought of as disposable."

Genie was taken aback by her wish. The woman before him spoke with such eloquence and passion, not of herself but of her fellow human beings. He could tell that she wasn't wishing this for selfish reasons—something to gain for herself at the expense of another. He was so overwhelmed with joy that he burst into laughter.

At first, Eleanor was stung by his laughter. He thought her a fool, a nincompoop, a joke, she gathered. She shrugged her shoulders and sighed. Disappointed that the male sex, even a magical one, thought little of her and her aspirations to do good in the world, she turned on her heels and walked away from Genie. She had genuinely wanted to help those less fortunate than her. Her husband had the power to do such things; people listened to him, but he had much greater responsibilities at the moment. She wanted to do her part. Although she didn't have the love she craved from her mother and she, herself, wasn't the best mother, her heart ached for the children suffering in the warehouses, working long, grueling hours, day after day, for mere pennies to help support their impoverished families. The women worked in the factories too. They were forced to work either because their husbands were killed in the war, or they were struck by the depression that had swept through the country. Neither the women nor the children had a voice. She desperately wanted to be their voice.

"Eleanor, please!" Genie cried out. "I do not belittle you! It's simply refreshing to hear those words uttered from you—not you personally, just someone not after their own personal agenda."

Eleanor returned to Genie. "I meant my wish, Genie," she said. "I have seen too much strife in my life, and it's usually in the hands of those in power. Well, I have the power, and I want to do well with what has been presented to me."

"Eleanor, I grant you your wish. I truly want this to come true for you. I know you will do well in this life you have been born and married into. But, if possible, do me this one favor for I do not know if your wish will come true. If it should happen that the wish cannot be granted now for future use, promise me you will do everything in your power to make it happen anyway," he begged.

"I intend to," she replied.

Satisfied, he continued, "What is your second wish and is this wish for now or for later?" he asked. "I do hope that you will make a wish that I can see its outcome. For far too long, I have been witness to the unspeakable. I would like to be able to grant a good wish for once that I can bear witness to with joy."

"Well, you see," Eleanor started to lay out the plans for her next wish. "I have always been a stubborn child. I think it's due to the fact that I had to grow up quickly when my parents died along with my brother. I lost the ability to laugh and find joy in the simple things. I do not pretend that I could be the most asked-for socialite in my circle, but I wish to have the ability to make friends. Not superficial friends," she corrected. "The kind of friends with meaningful relationships. The type of friends who share my desire for equality among women and those who did not have opportunities due to their status in life. I do not desire to talk for hours on end about the weather, I need a deeper connection."

"Is there a particular friendship with someone you have in mind that I can grant you now?" Genie desperately wanted to grant Eleanor's wish now. He longed for the peace of goodness that his curse could perceivably bring about. It was so close to him that he could almost taste the happiness.

Eleanor thought about the question posed to her.

*Who would I want to be friends with the most?* She contemplated. *Who would share my values and lofty, controversial ideas?*

Two names popped into her head.

"I wish to be friends with Nancy and Marion," she blurted out the names. "Now, I don't want these to be forced friendships. I want them to develop naturally, but I want some catalyst for us to join forces and do something spectacular. I know they would be willing to give it a go, but I just need to start with them."

There was a sudden knock at the door of Eleanor's room. She looked to Genie as if to ask him who it could be. He winked at Eleanor and gave her a sideways grin, knowing who had knocked.

Through unknown forces, Nancy and Marion waited on the other side of the door. When Eleanor opened the door, the two flew at her with questions cloaked in laughter. They told her, both speaking simultaneously, that they had been drawn to her house. The two met at the front gate of the house, bewildered why they were there but knowing they had to speak with Eleanor. Each had been struck with the idea of opening a finishing school for girls and partnering with Eleanor to purchase the Todhunter School. An endeavor they were sure would teach girls how to be more assertive in today's society, thus turning out strong-willed women at the tutelage of the three of them.

Genie beamed with pride as the young women spoke of lofty goals and ambitions hardly uttered in men's circles. These three strong females would set the tone for a new, equal world.

Listening as the group continued discussing their ideas, Genie glanced out the window to see the sun lowering in the sky. He could hear the women laughing, goodheartedly, at their ideas. His ears filled with high-pitched giggles, and he wanted to join in the fun. His heart was filled with joy and sorrow at the same time as he was to them. Eleanor hadn't made her third wish and time was drawing close to an end. Seeing Genie, Eleanor caught his attention away from the window. She knew Nancy and Marion couldn't see him, given that they expressed no surprise at his presence when they had entered the room. Casually, she strolled over to the window in a manner that suggested she was merely closing the curtains. The other two were too engaged in conversation to notice anything out of the ordinary. Eleanor bade Genie closer with her forefinger. He leaned in to hear her.

Without any fanfare or disruption to the scene behind her, she softly whispered to Genie.

"For my last wish, I wish for your freedom," she smiled at Genie as she watched him instantly disappear from her sight. Grinning to herself, she skipped over to join the conversation and unbridled laughter that was underway.

# 21
# GENIE'S REDEMPTION

U pon Eleanor's final wish, Genie was transported to a place he had never been. No longer was he sent to the familiar interior of the lamp. This place was dark, damp, and cold. He was standing in a massive interior room that appeared to be an underground cave carved into a stone palace of some sort. Polished grey, almost black stones made the floor and walls. Bronze light torches aligned the walls creating orange reflections on the stone floor. Directly in front of him were three steps that led to a platform. In the center of the platform was a stone-carved throne. Surrounding the throne were tall pillars with fire crackling at their apex.

Genie looked around the silent chamber. Nothing could be heard but the flames of the various fires. He started to look for an escape door when he realized he was standing—standing on two feet. His ghostly body had vanished. He was whole again. The thought of escape momentarily flew from his thoughts. He twirled around himself, looking at his solid form when suddenly Divine-Genie materialized on the throne.

"So, someone was kind enough to release you," Divine-Genie sneered. He didn't seem happy to see the man standing before him.

"Yes. I'm just as surprised as you are," he nervously laughed.

"I'm not surprised," Divine-Genie chuckled at Genie's naivety. "I'm enraged!"

Genie was confused by the displeasure of his Divine Maker. *Isn't this what all genies had wanted?* He wondered.

"Divine-Genie," he began. "Isn't this the ultimate goal? To be free? Free from the curse? To become mortal again?"

"For you, maybe. Not for me." He rose from the throne and floated towards Genie. "I made you, yes. I gave you a way out from your curse, yes. But I do not have the same luxury as you do. I am stuck in my prison forever. No one can grant me a wish for freedom. Genies are created to grant the wishes of mortals. Once you have become mortal again, you have no wishes. Therefore, you, or any other genie released from their bond, cannot grant wishes for me." Divine-Genie's wrath was apparent, but the underlying pain did not stem from anger, it stemmed from jealousy and hurt.

"I feel sorry for you." Genie spoke with sincerity and compassion. He felt Divine-Genie's pain. He may not have been a genie for as long as Divine-Genie had, but he knew what his internal struggles were.

"Do not pity me!" Divine-Genie screamed. "Do not dare to assume to know me. Do not dare to assume to know my thoughts. I cherish my power and would not give it up to become mortal again!"

"Your power?" Genie's eyes pierced the apparition with anger. "Your power? The power to fuel the wicked thoughts of mortals.

The power to cause pain and torture to innocent people. The power to inflict horror throughout society. You cherish that?"

"Oh, yes. Yes, I do. And so do you. I saw the way you struggled with the wishes you granted and how deep down you envied your masters. I saw how you wanted to hold those knives and cut into human flesh. I saw how you wanted to take women to satisfy your own lust. I saw it all. You cannot stand there and tell me you didn't feel that power. Didn't feel it surge through your once-human veins? You wanted it just as much as the masters you served," Divine-Genie spat.

Genie hung his head at Divine-Genie's words, reminding him of all he had done in his past. He was ashamed of his actions even though, for all his power, he was powerless to stop the others from their heinous acts. The reminder of his own desire to be the previous masters he served at the moment of committing those crimes stung him to his core. He hated himself for these feelings.

"Ah," Divine-Genie interrupted his self-loathing. "I see you struggle with your demons. They are still there. They will always be there, even in your mortal form. They will surface when you least expect it. They will eat at you. They will torment you until you release them. You cannot hide them no matter how hard you try. They are a part of you now."

"I will try," Genie whispered.

"You will fail," Divine-Genie retorted.

"I will try," Genie said more sternly as he looked at Divine-Gine again. "I will try to banish my demons. I will fight them with laughter. I will fight them by bringing joy to people. I will fight them with humor and good. I will fight them by making others forget their internal demons, even if it's just for an hour or two.

I will lock them deep inside me; forcing them to never surface again. You will see."

"Suit yourself," Divine-Genie shrugged.

"I've had enough of you and your vile comments. I have had enough of servitude to your disgusting whimsical voyeurism. Release me into the world now! Name me, as is the rule, and let me leave this place!"

Despite Divine-Genie's hesitation, he knew he had no choice but to release Genie. He was, and always would be, a slave to his prison. And he was comforted by the life he was condemned to. He enjoyed watching others suffer. Their suffering made him who he was. He had no such ambitions as the man before him to leave this place. The chains that kept him bound were his comfort.

"Have it your way," he grumbled. "Your name shall be Robin. Now, leave my sight." With that, Genie, now Robin, was transported into the human world.

Robin stood in front of a wooden structure turned into a bar. It was a hot spot for the San Francisco locals, and the crowds poured in on the weekends, ready for a night of fun. He had worked here for two years, schlepping beers to the patrons and listening to the Friday night improvs. He had watched with envy as the comics got up on stage, trying to make the audience laugh. Some were great. Some were horrible, but they had the courage to make a go at it. Tonight, it was Robin's turn. He had worked long after the bar had closed on his routine of jokes. Sitting in his tiny apartment, he scribbled and scratched jokes he thought would make people laugh.

Whispers of Jack, Vlad, and the others tried to creep into his thoughts. He pushed them away, burying them through his work. He cast them down into the pits of his soul; wielding the power of laughter until he couldn't hear them any longer.

He found humor in the current affairs of the country. He made jabs at the rich and famous. He even went so far as to talk about touchy subjects like relationships and his own childhood, but not so much that the quieted demons would jump upon the chance to surface again. He found a way to connect with those whose attention he wanted to capture. Now, it was time to put it all together and see what he could do. He cursed his demons when they tried to surface when he had doubts about his own ability. He needed to overcome them. He desperately needed to fill his life with the sounds of laughter. It took him many years of hard work to get to this point. Countless hours of classes on how to deliver his lines perfectly. Finding the right moments to pause. Finding the right comebacks for the hecklers. He was ready.

Pushing down those inner demons, the memories of his previous masters, and his own insecurities, Robin opened the door and took the stage.

# ABOUT THE AUTHOR

PT Bateman is a thrilling suspense writer residing in the picturesque state of Maryland, USA, where she shares her home with her four beloved rescue pets. From a young age, PT Bateman harbored an insatiable passion for storytelling and the written word, which eventually led her down the enthralling path of becoming a suspense novelist. While writing remains her true passion, PT Bateman is also a full-time employee, proving that determination and perseverance are the keys to unlocking one's dreams.

Despite the challenges of a busy professional life, she never loses sight of her commitment to her readers and the art of suspenseful storytelling. Outside of her literary pursuits, PT Bateman finds solace and joy in the wonders of gardening. Tending to her plants and flowers, she nurtures a connection with nature that mirrors the growth and evolution of her own characters. Additionally, her love for books extends beyond reading, as she takes pleasure in various book-related crafts, breathing life into her stories even beyond the confines of the written word.

Stay tuned for more heart-stopping adventures from PT Bateman, as she continues to push the boundaries of suspense fiction and leave an indelible mark on the literary landscape.

www.ingramcontent.com/pod-product-compliance
Lightning Source LLC
Chambersburg PA
CBHW040907010826
48978CB00013BB/1185